I0539770

The Funambulist

A Novella

by

Mark W. Lyon

Published by Mark W. Lyon

2972 Vale Court, Lake Oswego, OR 97034-7563 U.S.A.
www.markwlyon.us

Copyright © 2014 by Mark W. Lyon
All rights reserved. No part of this book may be reproduced, scanned, or
distributed in any printed or electronic form without permission.
ISBN-10: 0988797259
ISBN-13: 978-0-9887972-5-3

For Fred who lived this story
And Stephen who gave him new life

CONTENTS

THURSDAY

Finn Hauken released the handrail on the side of the aircraft, felt the air fill his wing suit, and then soared, blissful and free, on an ocean of sky where the Korean would never find him.

Cold wind rippled his face. Through the goggles he saw twelve parachutists below him maneuvering to begin practice for their upcoming competition. Finn adjusted his arms and legs, contouring the wing suit, and flew to a favorable position for his helmet camera to film the performance.

From Finn's perspective, his team executed their position changes brilliantly until two jumpers collided at six thousand feet. He watched them pull away in opposite directions and throw their pilot chutes. *Good move,* he thought. One canopy opened, abruptly stopping the parachutist's descent. Finn and the other jumpers hurtled past him in free fall and then Finn saw the second chute unfurl but not open. He recognized the jump suit: Andrea was in trouble. He'd trained everyone on his team to handle this mishap, but that didn't stop the rush of anxiety flaring up inside him. He flattened his body and sped toward her.

Finn closed on the slower falling Andrea and was relieved to see her moving methodically to correct the situation. *She's got plenty of time,* he thought, and watched her reach up and try to disentangle the lines. But the chute didn't respond. It continued to flap and flutter above her. *Cutaway!* he yelled silently.

Andrea wasn't a novice, but Finn knew she lacked the experience to estimate her remaining time aloft. Every second she hung below the failed chute, the ground seemed closer to her than it actually was and her terror of smashing onto the field and exploding into tiny pieces of blood and flesh grew exponentially. His jaw tightened as he watched her gestures become frantic and reckless. He stretched his body for more speed.

Finn drew closer and Andrea seemed to recover situational awareness. He saw her look down at the looming earth. Then at her altimeter. Up at the flapping canopy. She made another attempt to unravel the lines, again with no success. Finn's heart jumped when he saw her pull the D-ring to open her reserve chute without first detaching the main chute. *You didn't cutaway!* The two canopies intertwined and twisted uselessly above her.

We're running out of altitude. He dove toward the nylon swirling above her head and grabbed a handful as he sailed past but it tore from his hand. *Damn!* It seemed to take forever to maneuver into position for another pass.

He seized again. This time, his grip felt solid and he threw his own pilot chute. Finn's main popped a few hundred feet above the ground. He gritted his teeth and pulled one riser with his free hand. It steered them to the field and stalled his chute just in time.

Andrea tumbled onto the dry pasture. Finn sailed over her and landed, running on his feet. He shucked his parachute and raced to Andrea, hoping to hell she was unhurt. She got to her feet, dazed and wobbling. He took her arm.

"Andrea."

"Oh my God!" She looked at him. Her face was ashen and the muscles jerked spasmodically. Her eyelids beneath the goggles blinked out of sync.

"C'mon, lie down."

"Oh my God!"

Finn pulled her gently to the ground. "Let's be sure you're okay."

"Oh my God!" She couldn't stop her facial muscles from twitching, but she lay down.

From the hangar and the parked cars, people ran toward them.

~

Finn hated crowds, but he waited beside Andrea while one of the other jump masters, a paramedic, examined her. Having decided she displayed no sign of concussion, the medic told her to rest where she was and let the spasms subside over the next hour. The airport manager, Randy Powell, a squat old man with a loud voice and a clipboard, grilled the medic until he was satisfied that Andrea was unhurt. Then Finn saw Randy come toward him with his jaw set and eyes like an eagle. Negative publicity and extra paperwork never helped a parachute club or anyone else. Finn grabbed the offensive. "Randy, can you help me out here?"

"Sure, Finn," his face seemed to relax. "Anything."

"When you file the incident report with the Fed, can you leave my name out of it?"

"Geez, Finn," Randy had overcommitted. "That I can't do."

"Sure you can. Just say, the safety officer or the jump master or something like that."

Randy raised the clipboard like a shield. "Look, Finn. In the two years you've been here, you've become my best jump master and I'd like to help you. But you know the FAA, the USPA. They want manifests, names, certifications. If it's not all there, I'm out of business."

Finn put his hands on his hips, his brow furrowed. He felt Randy studying him. "Something I should know about, Finn?"

Finn looked down at Andrea lying on her back, watching them from a few feet away, and tried to relax the tension in his gut. Finally, his mouth softened into a smile and he turned to Randy and lowered his voice, adopting an easy, aw-shucks tone. "It's just . . . well . . . you know . . . ex-wife . . . be better she didn't know where I was."

Randy's eyes brightened and he lowered the clipboard. "Well hey, it's your lucky day. This report goes to the Fed, remember?" He shook the clipboard for emphasis. "Not like anybody actually reads this stuff."

Finn looked into Randy's eyes. "These things always find a way to go public."

"Nah, you worry too much." Randy put his hand on Finn's shoulder. "You're a hero, boy. You saved a girl's life. Thanks to you, she'll leave in her tennis shoes instead of a body bag."

"All the more reason the papers will get hold of it." Finn said. He looked hard at Randy. "Please don't use my name."

Randy withdrew his hand and let out a forced laugh. "World doesn't even know we exist out here, Finn. Relax. Go home. Take tomorrow off. Enjoy a three-day weekend. Be proud of what you did."

Finn took a deep breath and swallowed his frustration. He turned slowly and went to retrieve his chute, focusing his eyes on the ground two steps ahead and trying to ignore the dry feeling in his throat. He passed three jumpers who'd been watching him since they had landed.

"Awesome. Just awesome," said the first, loud enough for everyone to hear.

"Hey, Circus Dude, nice flying." The second was just as loud.

"World-class, man" said the third.

Finn tipped his head, pleased that they admired his skill, but their praise couldn't shake the worry that his life was about to change without his permission.

~

Finn stomped through the front door of the twenty-eight-foot Airstream and flung his jump bag on the vinyl couch. He clenched his fists, leaned on a counter in the galley, and stared out the window for a long time at the slice of Pope Valley visible through the trees. *How long before news gets out and someone sees my name? Then what? Call Philippe? Ask what to do next?*

The thought of calling his boss for help stopped Finn's train of thought. *Maybe Randy's right and nobody will ever find me here.* He opened the small refrigerator below the sink in front of him, transferred a package of bacon and a carton of eggs to the countertop, and set a skillet on the front burner. When the bacon grew fragrant, he broke four eggs into a bowl.

Behind him, his Golden Retriever, Mattie, galloped through the open door and sprawled onto the linoleum with a furious scraping of claws. Her tail thrashed the walls and toppled a wooden chair. When she finally reached Finn, she sat on his feet, lifted her nose up toward his face and fixed him with lustful eyes.

"Hello, girl." He reached down and scratched her head. "Smell something you like?" The words no sooner left his mouth than her ears twitched and she turned back to the door with a deep growl.

"Someone coming?" Finn whispered. Mattie trotted to the door and stopped, her tail low and still. Finn sprang off one foot, his body arced in the air toward the back of the trailer and alighted in front of the wardrobe without a sound. He slid open the top drawer and removed a Springfield XDM 45ACP. Holding the automatic in his right hand, arm dangling slightly behind his thigh, he stole back toward the front of the trailer, stopped beside Mattie, and waited.

The retriever made an ambiguous sound between a whine and a growl. Finn couldn't interpret the meaning. No one appeared on the path at the foot of the steps. Finn leaned right, looked out a window and scanned a section of the path that was hidden from the front door by a large madrona tree.

"Hello? Anyone here?" The proximity of the young female voice on the deck outside the window unsettled him. *How had she come so close?*

Mattie stood and growled. Finn set the automatic on the counter, dropped a towel over it, and grabbed Mattie's collar with his left hand. "Just us chickens," he said and stepped into the open doorway.

She stood in flip-flops, tan shorts and a sleeveless blouse, a young figure with a dancer's toned legs and a pretty blond pony tail loosely gathered high on the back of her head. Finn recalled that she had been cheerful and open during the jump classes but now, in the dappled sunlight, her eyes were cautious, her mouth tentative.

"I—I wasn't sure I should come," Andrea stammered. "I mean, I didn't know if you'd be here."

"No." Finn said. "I mean yes. It's fine. I'm glad you're all right." He dragged Mattie by the collar out of the doorway and stepped back to make room for the girl. "Come in. Your face looks a lot better now."

"Yeah?" She nodded and smiled. "I stayed by the hanger until I was, like, totally calm. Randy told me how to find you. I hope it's okay?" She stepped carefully into the trailer, saw Mattie straining in Finn's grasp and held her open palm out in greeting. Finn released the collar. Mattie lunged forward and gave the hand a cursory sniff before thrusting her nose into Andrea's crotch.

"Mattie!" Finn scolded. The dog instantly retreated.

Andrea looked up, unabashed, her smile once again cheery. "Smells really good in here. Are you cooking breakfast?"

"Yeah, all that zooming made me hungry," Finn grinned and cocked an eyebrow in her direction. "You too?"

"Sure." She glanced away and systematically scanned the Spartan interior. Finn waited until her eyes returned to his and she asked, "How long have you had this place?"

"Couple of years."

"You don't have much stuff."

He wanted to say it was so he could move quickly, but that would be too much information. "What's enough stuff?"

"You know, what most people have: furniture, plants, pictures on the wall, souvenirs of your travels, empty beer cans," she swept one arm around the bare room. "It's . . . It's so clean."

Finn laughed at her innocence. "Makes it easier when unexpected guests arrive. I don't have to rush around putting things in order."

She closed the distance between them. "Were you expecting anyone in particular?"

Her inviting aroma caught Finn off guard. "No," he couldn't help smiling. "I was just contemplating my future." He turned his head and gave her a sideways glance. "And preparing breakfast. You never know who'll turn up."

Her abrupt response surprised him. She wrapped both arms around his middle and laid her head against his chest. "I didn't come for breakfast."

Finn took a second to recover. Then he took Andrea's shoulders and looked down at her loosely bound hair. "Mm." He tipped her head back so he could look her in the eye. "You should probably know that I don't get close to people."

5

As if she hadn't heard a word he said, Andrea reached up with her hands, pulled their faces together, and devoured his lips. He sensed her state of mind, recognized the intensity of feeling that persists after a narrow escape from death. Honored it, in fact. One arm squeezed her close while his other hand reached back and shut off the flame under the bacon. Then he reached around her waist and held her firmly in both arms. She lifted her feet and encircled his body with her thighs. Finn rose immediately to the occasion. As she yielded in his arms, he entertained a conscious thought of carrying her to the bed, but his unconscious mind acted sooner. He sank with her to the floor and, with one hand, unbuttoned the white blouse and slipped it from her shoulders. She pulled the shirt over his head while he undid her tan shorts. Then he lifted her so she could close her legs and let him slide the shorts and underpants down her thighs, over her ankles. She unfastened his belt and he felt a rush of pleasure as she freed him from the jeans. A piercing sound, like a submarine dive klaxon, filled the room.

The phone. He groaned. His entire body went slack. He felt her tense and he rolled them to one side. "I'm sorry. I've got to take this."

"What?" Big frown.

"It's a special number. I can't ignore it. I'm really sorry." Finn stood and grabbed the phone off the counter and saw her roll away toward Mattie. The caller ID showed, UNKNOWN. Someone could have misdialed his number, but Finn couldn't take that chance. He drew the phone to his ear.

"Finn?" asked a tremulous voice. He recognized Emma Kassar, his boss's wife.

"Emma."

"I need your help."

Finn let the phone fall to his side and stared at Andrea, now sitting naked, with her back to him, stroking Mattie's exposed belly, her tanned muscles rippling with the movement. Her left breast, the one he could see, undulated when she leaned forward. He wanted more than anything to toss the phone and continue their exploration, but he couldn't. He pressed it to his ear.

"What's the matter with Philippe this time?"

"Philippe is dead."

Finn's jaw dropped. "Jesus. I'm sorry."

Andrea heard his concern and stopped playing with the dog.

"He was on a trip." Emma stated. "They think he was murdered."

Murdered! Finn was stunned. "Well, that sucks."

Andrea looked at him over her shoulder. Her brow wrinkled.

"Are you all right?" Finn said into the phone.

"No," Emma's voice filled with emotion. "I'm afraid. I don't know what's going to happen . . . what to do . . . the business . . . the police. I need someone I can trust. That's why I called."

"What a God damned nightmare." Finn tried to picture Philippe, always so effervescent, now a pale corpse.

"It's worse than that."

He saw Andrea retrieve her blouse and shorts, felt a swell of disappointment as she began to dress. He turned and walked toward the bedroom. "You want me there, I guess?"

"The sooner the better."

He would be exposing himself in San Francisco. Finn lowered his voice. "Philippe told me to lay low until he called."

"Philippe is dead, Finn. I'm calling you."

"What about the Chinese?"

"Things have calmed down since you left. They won't bother you."

"The police think I killed Younger Park."

"Oh Finn. Forget it. You can prove that you didn't kill Younger Park."

"But his brother thinks I did."

"Holliday's vanished. Nobody's seen him in over a year."

Finn paused. He looked over his shoulder at Andrea fixing her pony tail. "I don't know."

"Philippe could always count on you to do the right thing," she retorted.

Damn! Finn exhaled, a long note of resignation. He lowered the phone and let his right thumb absently caressed a small tattoo on the inside of his left wrist. He was trapped. He owed Emma. She had brought her husband to watch Finn fight a mixed martial arts tournament in Daley City years ago. His circus training gave him the edge over a more skilled opponent. Philippe had hired him on the spot and had provided the time and money to elevate his fighting skills to a level he'd never imagined possible, and, most important, the opportunity to wield them fiercely and often.

Philippe respected Finn's aversion to killing people and his own taciturn disposition had encouraged Philippe to make him his sole confidant. The man was a genius, a first class crook, but he was Finn's friend and mentor. Now he was dead. *I can't believe it*. Still, he owed him. Even in the grave, Philippe would want him to help his wife. He brought the phone up to his ear and prayed he would survive the next few days.

~

In her luxurious home in the Forest Hill neighborhood of San Francisco, Emma Kassar perched on a stool in a kitchen festooned with culinary equipment and worried about her future. With her husband dead, her income was gone. Operating Philippe's business was beyond her abilities. On the plus side, their joint bank account would see her through the next year. And Finn had agreed to come to San Francisco. At least that was easy. Even her deceased husband could manipulate him. She smiled at the thought and sipped from her coffee cup. On the other hand, convincing him to stay the course while she extricated Philippe's business from its contracts, paid off the shareholders, and unshackled herself from further obligation was another matter. Finn was notoriously impetuous but once given direction, unstoppable until he'd achieved his goal. As long as he believed she was vulnerable, he would remain by her side.

Emma took another sip from her coffee and picked up her iPhone. She held down the home button on the phone and when she heard two beeps said, "Call my brother."

~

The smartphone vibrated on the wooden nightstand with the irritating buzz that heralds bad news. It disoriented Dan Emmonds. He knew he'd disabled the ringer and couldn't imagine the source of the noise. His confusion cleared and he grabbed the phone after the first ring, checked the caller ID, and held it to his ear.

"Emma?" After a second, he added in a hushed voice. "Sure. Where are you? Be right there," Dan said quietly. The clock on the nightstand said 8:30. He swung his legs out of bed, trying not to wake Myrna, his girlfriend du jour, and tiptoed to the bureau for his clothes. Five minutes later, he came out of the bathroom fully dressed. Myrna's cobalt blue eyes stared boldly into his.

"Who was on the phone?" she asked.

"My sister, Emma. Something happened to Philippe. I gotta go."

"What happened?"

"She said he was dead."

"Get out!" she said and rose up on her elbows. The sheet fell away from her elegant breasts and Dan had to remind himself that he'd told Emma he was on his way. He gathered his wallet and phone from the nightstand.

"I can't believe it either. I don't know what to think."

"Don't think!" Her voice sounded harsh. He ignored the tone and kissed her goodbye. As he shut the bedroom door he saw Myrna reach for her phone. He couldn't help his curiosity. *I only need a second.* Dan stopped outside to listen.

"Something's happening," her voice came through the door. There was a long pause. "Well, pardon me, Mister Know-It-All." Her tone shocked him. "Just trying to oblige." He heard the phone smash into the wall and decided he would wait until later to ask who she had called.

~

Emma leaned against her late husband's hand-carved desk and prepared herself to meet the most challenging day of her life.

Philippe's magnificent suite on the northeast side of San Francisco's sixth tallest building, 101 California Street, looked out from the forty-fifth floor onto the Embarcadero and the San Francisco Bay. Xanthus Investments was the realization of his long-held desire to own a prestigious and profitable enterprise. But for now, Emma ignored the spectacular view and attended her red face and uncombed hair in the mirror of a round compact. When Dan finally arrived, she lowered the mirror and waited for him to come around the desk and embrace her. They held each other in silence.

After a few moments, Emma pulled away and took a deep breath.

"Some policewoman called from Italy. I could barely understand her. Except —" Tears flooded her eyes, "Philippe is dead and I'm all alone."

"I'm here," Dan sounded reassuring.

Emma let her shoulders relax. "I know, thank you."

"Did she say what happened?"

"No, damn it! I have no idea! Just that he's dead."

Dan stepped back. "Whoa, easy."

"Sorry. It's just—"

"Okay. Don't worry."

Tears returned to her eyes. She listened to Dan's soothing tone.

"Hey, what do you need? What can I do? What about Philippe's body?"

She tried to concentrate. "I don't know yet. I'm still trying to figure everything out." Then she turned to him. "Could you manage Philippe's workload for a while?"

"Yes, I can do that," he said.

"There are two items that need attention right away." Thinking about the business at hand brought her thoughts into focus. "First, we have to move quickly with the BrighTel sale coming up on Monday."

Dan nodded. She lifted a Post-it note free of the desktop and scanned it. "Second, an investigator from the Bureau of Industry and Security? Part of the

Commerce department? He contacted Philippe. Something to do with export licenses."

"No problem" he offered. "Anything else? Anyone we need to contact?"

"I already called Logan Evans," she said and noticed Dan raise his eyebrow. "He should know what's going on. He's our main shareholder." Emma glanced at her watch. It read 9:00 o'clock. "Also, the police are coming any minute. They have questions."

~

Detective Ariel Hedges followed Xanthus' receptionist into an office so spacious and commanding that hairs tingled on the back of his neck. *This one's all about money*, he thought. The receptionist backed out of the room after announcing his name and closed the door. An athletic blond man in his thirties—the brother, he assumed—stepped forward with his hand extended. Hedges took it and nodded. He turned to the dark haired woman standing beside the desk, and felt the allure of her brown eyes touch him even through her red and swollen face. He reached out and handed Emma his card.

"Missus Kassar," he said, accompanying his deep voice with a formal bow. "I'm very sorry about your husband."

Emma ran her eyes over the card before dropping it on the desk. When she looked at him again, her face had acquired a careless, neutral expression. "Thank you, detective."

"Yes, m'am," he said. They shared a moment of respectful silence before Hedges continued, "There are some things I need—"

She cut him off. "The woman who called . . . I couldn't understand . . . I mean . . . What happened?"

Hedges tried to look sympathetic. "The Italian police say your husband was stabbed during a robbery."

"What did they take?" Dan interjected.

"His jewelry and smartphone were missing, but they're not sure whether anything else is." Hedges turned to the brother, saw him shake his head to show what he thought of the Italian police.

"They want our help with this case, so they're sending a liaison to speed up the flow of information." He let the sound of his deep voice convey his mastery of the situation. "In the meantime, I just need to ask a few questions. Can we sit? It won't take long."

They found seats, Emma behind the desk, Dan in one of the leather chairs by the glass coffee table, Hedges in the other leather chair. The detective removed a small notebook and ball point pen from inside his suit coat. He gave the pen a purposeful click and looked at Emma.

"Anyone who might want to harm your husband?"

They both shook their heads.

"Who besides Philippe was involved in Xanthus?"

"Just Emma and a few private investors," Dan said. "People Philippe knew."

The detective nodded and looked at Emma. "Kassar. Lebanese, right?"

Emma acknowledged with a smile.

"Any other foreign-born nationals involved in Xanthus?"

"Why do you ask?" She looked puzzled.

"Mister Kassar was killed outside the country," Hedges replied. "Just covering all the bases."

"No," Emma said. "We used to have a Korean investor, but not for the last two years."

"What happened to him?"

"He passed away."

"May I get a list of shareholders?"

"The receptionist will have it when you leave," Emma said.

"Xanthus does venture capital, right?" Hedges raised his eyebrows, looking innocent.

"Private investment," she corrected. "Overseas trading. Import financing— although I'm not sure I really understand all of that."

"Do you know the company's net worth?"

"Around $40 million, Philippe said once," Emma told him.

Hedges made a note, just for something to do. "How many employees?"

"About thirty," Emma said.

"Either of you left the area recently?" He asked.

They both shook their heads.

"Know anyone in Italy?" he continued, looking at Emma.

Again, both heads signaled, no.

"Could a thief have wanted anything else from Mister Kassar besides jewelry and electronics?"

"Philippe was going for only a few days," Emma said. "He just took clothes."

"You stayed behind?" His tone was surprised.

"He liked to be alone when he was considering a new investment," Emma said.

"Is that what he was doing?"

"Yes," Emma said. "A client wants funds to acquire mobile phone spectrum from the government."

"What did he have to consider?"

"Probably where to get the money."

Hedges looked at Emma, then at Dan. "Anything else I should know? Anyone else we should be concerned about?"

They both shook their heads. *Well, everyone's innocent, apparently,* Hedges suppressed a smirk and stood to leave.

~

Although Finn lucked out catching an early flight from Santa Rosa, he still had to wait for a connecting flight in Seattle and wouldn't make San Francisco until rush hour. From a seat at one of the myriad Starbucks in SEATAC, he stared into the river of humanity flowing along the C concourse and felt himself ascending from the lethargy of Napa County into the turbulence of enforcing the wishes of his former boss. A familiar tension grew inside him: eagerness to act, to move, to make things happen. It just aggravated his frustration. His fingers tightened around the coffee cup.. *Philippe is dead and I'm stuck in Seattle.*

Finn drank the last of his coffee and decided he could do nothing to get himself to San Francisco any sooner. Thinking about Philippe made him sad and confused. Better to look ahead.

Obviously, someone killed Philippe for money. No one liked him much, but no one hated him enough to waste karma killing him. Check that. Roscoe maybe hated him that much. Roscoe believed to his core that Philippe stole Xanthus from him. Wasn't true but he could see Roscoe's point. Philippe had turned the modest import-export business into a cash machine and then sidelined Roscoe by purchasing the firm's majority interest from its founder, Holliday Park. *We best look in on Roscoe.*

Who else? Logan Evans? Holliday had sold Evans the minority interest in Xanthus after his brother, Younger, was murdered. Logan had profited richly from the deal, but Philippe kept him out of the real business. Logan knew about the high interest loans to Chinese importers. After all, that was their main activity. But Philippe didn't let on about the exorbitant fees Finn collected when they couldn't pay on time. *Had Logan found out about the fees?*

Maybe one of the Chinese forwarders finally had it with Philippe. But Emma said things had calmed down since the early days when he'd fought the Chinese hard and bloody to collect Xanthus' debts. *Hmm, not so likely, the Chinese.*

Well, shoot. Not many people left. Holliday Park himself? But the Korean hadn't been involved with Xanthus since his brother was killed. He and Philippe had an ongoing arrangement to service the Koreans. And Philippe had told him that Holliday wanted no harm to come to Roscoe. Not that Finn was afraid of Holliday, although he had a fearsome reputation. He avoided crossing the Korean because he knew Holliday felt obliged to Roscoe for once saving his life. Unfortunately, Holliday was also convinced that Finn had killed his brother and he wanted revenge. Still, that was Finn's problem, one that weighed heavily on him every day. But it had nothing to do with Philippe's death. And anyway, Holliday had gone missing for the past year.

What else? Finn could only speculate that Philippe had become involved in some new enterprise that had backfired and he'd have to find out what it was. *But first, checkout Roscoe and Logan.*

~

The question seemed to explode inside Logan Evans' bald head the instant Emma Kassar told him Philippe was murdered. *Does she know about the money he took?* Now in retrospect, he thought, if that was true, maybe she knew how much Philippe had squirreled away. More important, maybe she knew where it was. But then why had she told him Xanthus was going to honor its commitments? Why bother if she had the money? Why not just abandon the whole thing and disappear?

Because she doesn't know about the money!

He calmed down and drummed his thin fingers on the steering wheel of the Lexus. He waited in the left-turn lane, watching for a break in the continuous blur of oncoming cars. A gust of cold wind swung the traffic signals on the overhead cable and, finally, the green left-turn arrow changed to yellow and the approaching traffic slowed. The arrow turned red. The cross traffic rolled. Logan stomped the accelerator. The Lexus shot into the intersection, through the shrinking gap in the cross traffic and squealed around the corner inches ahead of a glistening black Pontiac. The driver was pissed and it made Logan smile. He loved to gamble. No, he loved to win.

Logan slowed for the next signal and felt his phone ring. He flipped on the Bluetooth speaker and saw the caller ID: Kishore Menon.

"Kishore," he said with gusto. "How's my favorite numbers guru?"

"Fine," replied a languid Indian voice. "Do you have a minute?"

"Sure. Go."

"I ran the income statement you wanted. I don't see how you can pay the pension-fund note next week."

Logan thought for a second. "What about Appleby?"

"We divested that one ages ago. Haven't you been paying attention?"

"Yeah." The light changed and the Lexus pulled away from the intersection. Logan caught himself. "No. I don't recall. Sorry. What about the equipment leases?"

"You would be losing 7.6 percent from the penalties for early termination."

"The Talus Bay Development property?" Logan knew he was fishing.

"The value has diminished 37 percent since you acquired it in 2010. It is underwater as you say." Menon's voice offered no hope. Logan stayed quiet for a long time.

"Damn, Kishore. Does it have to be next week?"

"I told you when you took the note, Logan, that these people will give you no wiggle room."

"I had something working, but it fell apart."

"I don't think they will accept that excuse." The speaker was quiet for a few moments then Menon said, "Did you tell me Xanthus was acquiring a telecom firm?"

Logan chuckled at the coincidence. "The guy spearheading that thing died yesterday."

Another pause. Then, "I'm very sorry to hear that, Logan."

"Yeah. Too bad. But we're considering alternatives."

"I hope you can find another way."

"I'm on my way now, Kishore. I'll call you later."

Logan turned into a parking garage. He circled down the cold concrete ramp and felt a sudden chill in the back of his throat. Maybe he was getting a cold. Maybe he was worried about making the pension fund payment. Or maybe he was just nervous about meeting Holliday Park for the first time.

~

Holliday searched the restaurant for a man he'd never met. The only single diner, a bald guy in a grey suit, was sitting alone fiddling with his water glass. *Must be him.* Holliday crossed the room without a sound and slid into the chair opposite Logan. When the broker finally saw him, he jerked involuntarily, spilling his water.

The reaction pleased Holliday, but he kept his face a mask of stone. His voice came out hard and direct. "Philippe is dead. What are you going to do now?"

Logan recovered quickly. "Is there anything you don't know?"

Park ignored the question. "His wife cannot run Xanthus. The person in charge must understand the clients. The biggest ones, the high tech companies, depend on Xanthus for trading between the US and Korea."

Logan nodded. "She knows nothing about that."

"You cannot let Xanthus fail. It has contracts with important customers. They require special attention." Park studied Logan to see if he was reading between the lines, if, indeed, he knew all about the business.

"I don't involve myself in day-to-day operations," Logan said. "But Philippe told me that our main income came from the Chinese."

"No." Park slammed the table with his palm. "That was Philippe's idea. He wanted to expand so he went after the traders for China. There are more of them than there are for Korea. But Xanthus' most important customers are Korean traders."

"I didn't know that," Logan lowered his eyes.

"Xanthus was created for Korean traders. I gave Roscoe control and Younger a minority share so he could monitor Roscoe's activity. Roscoe performed. I trusted him. When Philippe bought out Roscoe, Younger kept his shares and we kept some control. I came to trust Philippe. We found an arrangement. Then Younger died and Roscoe said you would be a good partner. I sold you my brother's share, even though we'd never met. But now that Philippe is dead, I have lost control. Yet, I must make certain that Xanthus will continue to serve the Koreans." Park stopped and waited for Logan's reaction, waited for his agreement.

A faint smile appeared on Logan's thin lips. "What do you have in mind?"

"Put Roscoe back in charge," Park snapped. "He's a licensed broker, US citizen, and he knows the customers." Logan's eyes opened wide. Then he looked down at the table and shook his head.

"He doesn't have the money."

"I know."

"Well then?"

"You will loan him the money."

"What?"

Park let a gleam into his eyes. "It's in your interest, Logan. Xanthus pays you good dividends."

"Yes, but—"

"If Roscoe takes over the company, I will guarantee Xanthus will continue to reward you for many years to come. Maybe even increase your share. But if Roscoe does not take over, we will all be like baby turtles dropped into a steaming broth."

"What makes you think I have the money to loan Roscoe?"

"Logan, money is your business. You will find it." Holliday was surprised suddenly to see a pleading expression come into Logan's eyes.

"Mister Park, Roscoe is a depraved freak."

Holliday sat up straight and laughed. "He does have quirks." Holliday thought back to a night in Gdansk. The orange lights on Tkacka Street. The surprise when half dozen locals attacked him and his friend. They fought hard. He'd survived the streets in Vladivostok. But the Poles were too many. He shuddered at the desperation he'd felt laying on his back. Bodies pinning him down. The terror that they would slit his throat. But suddenly, the bodies cleared. He glimpsed a giant standing above them, grabbing and pulling. Destroying the vandals with his huge fists. He owed his life to Roscoe. He recalled how happy he was when the promise of easy money and fast living persuaded Roscoe to come to San Francisco and be part of his family's import-export business.

"Roscoe had two vices when I met him," he told Logan. "Cold Polish vodka and soft Polish women. But he abused both and the basketball team in Gdynia sent back to America." Holliday's eyes narrowed. "But I trust him in business. He is the best person to run Xanthus."

~

Detective Hedges craned his head over the raucous crowd waiting outside the exit from Customs and Immigration. He searched the throng of arrivals on the 4:00 pm Alitalia flight for the man sent by the Carabinieri from Sienna. He had no clue what the police liaison looked like. *I'll bet he's special.* Whatever. He could handle it. Only one more week and he'd be gone to L.A. A promotion. Better department. Better pay. *Let's make this one easy.*

Hedges waited. After twenty minutes, he was alone, studying the half dozen passengers still milling around with their luggage carts. None of them looked likely. He glanced around for a white courtesy phone in order to leave a message. Knew I should have brought a sign. Hedges scan stopped when he saw the only unaccompanied woman in the group step boldly toward him.

"Scuzi, signore. You are Detective Edges?" Her blond hair was pulled into a bun. She wore striking clothes and sounded very sure of herself, more than her youthful appearance suggested.

This will be interesting. "Inspector Volpati?"

"Yes. Avvocatessa Allegra Volpati."

He gave her a smile and a formal bow. "You are a lawyer."

"Yes, I argue in the lower courts," she spoke in a low register with little emotion.

Hedges nodded. "Welcome to America, Miss Volpati."

Her eyes flashed briefly. "Please call me Allegra."

"The message said 'A. Volpati.' I was expecting a man."

"No. Is just me. First time here."

"Would you like coffee? Help the jet lag."

"Yes, thank you." Hedges took her suitcase and they strolled down a corridor towards Starbucks.

"Where in Italy do you come from, Allegra?"

"I am from a small village north of Bergamo near Milano. Do you know it?"

"I have been to Milan."

She turned to him with a wan smile. "Milano is where I go to school, Bocconi University."

"Have you been practicing long?"

"I have five-year school for *Magistrale in Giurisprudenza*. You call it master degree in justice. Now I make my eighteen-month apprenticeship with the *Pubblico Ministero*. You call him public prosecutor. When there is a crime in my country, he must find evidence of guilt or innocence. There is also chief inspector Romero in Sienna. I believe he contact you already?"

Hedges nodded. He noticed a young man with a knapsack over one shoulder fall in step beside Allegra. He was talking on his phone and moving with exceptional grace. Perhaps that's what caught her attention. Hedges heard him tell the phone that his dog ate once a day Allegra looked at the man. He glanced sideways at her and winked. Hedges saw her blush. The man spoke into his phone and Hedges heard him clearly. "Yeah, thanks for looking in on her, Andrea. We'll settle up when I get back." He laughed at something Andrea said and picked up his pace. After putting the phone in his pocket he looked back at Allegra with a beguiling smile. Allegra's eyes sparkled.

"We've got all kinds here," Hedges declared as the grinning man pirouetted with a flourish, then rose to his toes and sauntered away, clowning for Allegra's benefit.

"Look how he walk," Allegra guffawed and pointed a finger. "Like *funambolo*." She caught Hedges puzzled look. "Man in circus who walk on rope."

"Of course. A funambulist," Hedges nodded.

"Yes, is a tightrope." Her eyes followed the man until he was out of sight.

They joined the end of the line for Starbucks. Hedges offered to get both coffees while Allegra sat at a table, but she preferred staying on her feet after the long flight.

"So, Avvocatessa," the detective said after they advanced two places. "What do they say in Chianti? With an iPhone missing, I thought theft of information. Like, it implicated someone in a crime. Or identified the location of some stolen money. Something like that."

"Chief inspector Romero believe that person from America paid person in Italy to murder Mister Kassar," Allegra said.

"Really?" the detective looked surprised. "I thought it was burglary."

"Before Mister Kassar die, he was in restaurant with two men we call *teppisti* . . . hoodlum? Is the right word?"

Hedges nodded like he knew.

"They are from Siena. They do bad things for money."

"Interesting," speculated the detective. "Or perhaps a person from here went there to kill him."

Now Allegra looked surprised. "Why would person do that?"

"If someone wanted him dead, it's cleaner. Involves fewer people. Kassar's outside the country. Makes it harder for us to find the killer. Why else?" The cashier offered to take their order. "Two espressos," Hedges held out a twenty.

"But we would have immigration record in that case."

Hedges turned to her. "Fake passport?"

She reconsidered. "He was that kind of man? Someone people want dead?"

Hedges pocketed his change. "He was no saint." Allegra took the paper cup from his hand and he added, "Please pass my suspicions along to detective Romero."

~

Emma spent most of the day going through Philippe's things, trying to organize his papers, separating his belongings into piles: one to keep, one to distribute to friends, one to discard. Otherwise, she spent long periods pacing around the large office in mindless circles or staring out the windows at the fog swirling through the Bay Bridge.

By the end of the day, she'd she had enough of archeology. She locked Philippe's legacy behind the heavy wooden door of his office and went to find Dan. He sat in the conference room studying a dozen ledgers spread on the large walnut table. He was deep in concentration. She stood in the doorway and poked an arm through her coat sleeve, shifted her purse to the empty hand and waited.

"It's 5:00," she said, after he failed to notice her. Dan surfaced gradually. When he looked at her, she said, "I'm beat. I'll see you in the morning."

Dan shuffled papers around the desk as if he was looking for something. "Are these records up to date?"

"I gave you all of Philippe's books," she said. "But I'll check again in the morning. Right now, I can't. I'm too whipped."

She withdrew from the doorway.

"Be careful," Dan advised.

"Don't worry so much."

~

"Where's Emma?" Finn demanded when he found Dan working at the conference table. "I just checked Philippe's office and the door's locked."

Dan's head came up from the papers. His eyes stared at him with no recognition. Finn waited.

Eventually, Dan placed him. "Hello Hauken. What are you doing here?"

"Looking for Emma."

"You just missed her. She went home."

"Damn." Finn lowered his backpack to the floor. "She drive or take BART?"

"BART. But she'll probably eat first. Don't think she'll get home before 11:00."

Finn leaned against the door jam and surveyed the piles of paper. *He must be helping her with the books*, he concluded. Dan ran a successful accountant service from his home, so that made sense. Otherwise, he was a harmless geek, though an overly protective one. Probably why Dan had such a hard-on for him.

"You come because of Philippe?" Dan had put down his pen and placed both palms on the table.

"She asked me to."

Dan turned his head away. "My sister never learns from her mistakes, does she?"

"She needs help."

"Right." Dan looked back at Finn. "So she called you. The guy who gets sent away because he brutalizes the Chinese and they want to chop him up into wontons. Oh, don't look so surprised. I heard all about it."

Finn didn't know his face had registered surprise.

"You don't think that will be a problem?"

"No. I don't. Emma said things had quieted down with the Chinese." In truth, Finn wasn't entirely sure he was safe from an ambush by that quarter and intended to keep a low profile.

"I just don't know, Hauken. Never understood why she fell in love with you. She always liked guys that looked dangerous. But you? You're always walking through a war zone. I thought she would see that. But she didn't. You let her down, Hauken and I don't think she got over it. Even after she married Philippe."

Finn just stared back at Dan. He felt no shame. Heard it before. The truth was somewhat different although it still left plenty of room for him to feel humiliated and remorseful. *Damn I hate this. It's hard enough trying to shut off the past without people shoving it back in my face.*

"I just hope you didn't come here because Philippe is dead and you saw an opportunity to screw with her mind." Dan gave him a hard stare. Finn returned the look and let his mind go blank.

"I came to help her over this rough patch. Then I'm gone." Before Dan could reply, Finn added, "My job right now is to make sure nothing happens to her. Do you know where she went to eat?"

"I told you everything I know, Hauken."

Clearly, the man would be no further help. Finn picked up his knapsack. "Guess I'll catch her at home," he said and left the office.

~

Why didn't Philipe wrap up the BrighTel deal before he left for Italy? Emma asked herself. She reached for the carafe, exhaled loudly, and watched the garnet-colored liquid flow into her wine glass. *Things would now be so much easier.* She brought the glass to her lips. As it is, Xanthus will have to give them its cash reserves. How else will they be able to buy radio spectrum from the Fed? I don't like it. Leaves us vulnerable until the BrighTel spectrum sells. Philippe would never have done it this way. What was he thinking?

The waiter interrupted her train of thought. Set her meal on the table. Picked up the carafe and added more wine to her glass. She watched him walk away. *Don't these people pay attention?* she mused. A picture of her brother huddled over the conference table came to her mind. Why's he worried whether the ledgers are up to date? What's he finding in the books that I don't know about? Emma looked down at the duck breast before her and picked up her silverware.

Finn, damn it. Where's Finn? He should have been here by now.

~

A harbinger flitted in and out of Finn's head. Whether it was danger or anticipation, he couldn't tell and put it out of mind. He walked briskly through the Castro District, the epicenter of gay life in San Francisco for as long as anyone cared to remember. The streets pulsed with traffic, the sidewalks with pedestrians, their bodies, faces and fashions embellished beyond imagination.

The chilling fog rushing in from the Pacific ocean in late afternoon, blasting over Twin Peaks and enveloping the Castro in a misted shroud, lingering still at 10:00 pm. Finn moved quickly along the sidewalk weaving among couples of mixed ages, genders, and ethnicity. He headed for a familiar retreat on the fringe of the Castro to see an old friend, a neighborhood bartender. He stopped on Sixteenth, near the Roxie Theater, an area of typical San Francisco architecture, its buildings a hodge podge of businesses and residences, and peered through a large window into the cozy lounge of the Panama Hotel.

He watched the crowd inside, a mixture of cultures, races, and lifestyles typical for this part of town. The young and upscale filled the big leather chairs. They huddled around the standalone gas fireplace. Behind the fireplace, more trendies drank and talked in a space that might have hosted darts had the crowd been smaller. A bar to the right had a dozen stools, enough for one bartender, and a waitress station on the end closest to the lounge. The room looked inviting. Finn pulled open the door.

Only two steps into the lounge, he heard a female voice call him by name. He turned to his left and saw a slender girl in jeans and a bulky sweatshirt standing apart from the crowd. Her hair was tied back and she wore black framed glasses. His brain flashed, *librarian.* Then he recognized Teb. She paced the five steps between them, slowly removing her glasses and untying her hair. She was quite beautiful. Shiny walnut-colored hair, brown skin. The sense memory of the figure beneath her loose sweatshirt whirled through his mind.

"Finn. I haven't seen you in, like, ages." Her voice was frank, but her eyes sparkled.

"Teb." Finn looked down at her with a warm smile. "You're the first friendly face I've seen since I got back."

"Where you been?"

"Oh, you know, here and there."

She looked away for a second and then back into his eyes. "You need a place to crash?"

Finn smiled. "I do. Thank you. I would love to stay with you, but there's something I've got to do first. It'll take me about an hour. Can I come after?"

"Nothing that's going to use all your energy, I hope. I'm ready for another session in the Hauken school of gymnastics."

Finn laughed. "No. Just look in on a friend. Make sure she's all right."

Teb's eyes lost their sparkle. "Well Finn, if it's something important . . . I mean —"

"No. It's not like that." Finn saw his hopes for the evening fade. "She needs my help. But I don't, you know, have to stay and hold her hand or anything. If she's okay, then I'm gone."

Teb searched his face. It seemed like a long time before she spoke again. "Finn," she reached out and took his hand. "If it's important for you to help her, then you need to see it through."

"It'll be fine, Teb. Besides, I'd—"

"Finn," she smiled. "You know where I live. Just go do your stuff and don't worry about having to be someplace."

He retrieved his hand and drew her into a hug, felt the heat from her body. "Thanks, Teb." He released her and turned toward the bar, toward the reason he'd come here.

~

Finn eased his way through the room, feeling somewhat uncomfortable in the dense crowd. He was taking his time, respecting people's space, when a man in a 49ers baseball cap stumbled through the crowd and threw himself on Finn with a clumsy embrace. They stumbled and fell into the nearby patrons, spilling their drinks. Finn's hands sought a grip on anybody, but found none and he fell to the floor on his back with the other man lying on top of him.

He tried to push the drunk off, but the man clung to him with his head buried in his chest. Finn pushed harder. No response. Finally, he grabbed the man's ears in both hands and pushed his head away from his chest. The idiot looked at him and grinned.

"Sorry, man," slurred the drunk. "I must have slipped."

Until he saw the grin, Finn was ready to let it pass.

"Listen, asshole," Finn's eyes were cold and his voice could have fractured rock. "Get the fuck off me. Get your shit together and get the fuck out of this bar."

The idiot kept grinning, but he pushed himself off of Finn.

"What's the matter with you?" Finn asked, rising to his feet and regarding the grin, which now seemed contemptuous as well.

"Hey, friend," said a thin voice close behind Finn. "Why don't you take it easy? Can't you see the man's drunk?"

Finn turned around slowly. The crowd backed away, leaving a small circle for the two men: Finn and The Voice. An Asian, though not cast to type. A tall, muscular guy in head-to-toe leather, except for his cue-ball head and bulging arms. Finn gave him just half a second.

"You got a dog in this hunt, Nancy?"

The Voice tensed his upper body and threw a straight right fist at Finn's head. *Good punch.* Finn stepped to one side. The fist whipped past his face, the right arm stopped at the end of its travel, Finn snatched the wrist in his left hand with an iron grip and brought it down in front of him. Before the Voice could yank his hand away or launch another blow, Finn reached his right hand over the trapped fist, grabbed the thumb and yanked it backwards. There was a sickening snap and The Voice screamed in pain. Finn let go and watched him sink to his knees clasping both hands before his agonized face.

"Hey, Finn," the bartender shouted. "You're making a mess over there. Cut it out, will ya? Everyone was having a good time. Let's pick it back up, folks. Next round's on the house."

The crowd milled around, back to their places in the room. Finn watched The Idiot help The Voice limp out the front door. When he turned to go to the bar, the onlookers opened a path.

Jeff beamed from behind the bar. He was thick and tall with dark hair and full beard that accentuated the cuddly bear image he cultivated with his female clientele.

Finn smiled back at the familiar face.

"About time you showed up," Jeff extended his hand.

"Got thirsty."

"I didn't know you there for a second, 'til you pulled that thumb trick."

"Well, it's been a while," Finn paused. "You been having any fun?"

Jeff waved a hand around at the crowded room. "You can see we started without you."

"Rude as ever."

"Usual?"

"Bring it on."

Jeff took a bottle of Hirsch Selection Small Batch Reserve from the top row of the backbar. He placed a cut crystal glass in front of Finn and filled it half full. "Your name's still on this bottle."

Finn smiled at Jeff. "Have one yourself."

Jeff retrieved a second crystal glass for himself and filled it with an equal volume of the pricy bourbon. He set the bottle on the bar and lifted his glass to Finn. "Honored. Good to have you back."

They clinked, sipped, and said nothing for several minutes. *So much for incognito,* Finn said to himself.

~

"So, you here on a mission, or what?"

"Yeah," Finn replied without looking up. "Philippe Kassar, the guy I worked for? He died."

Jeff's jaw dropped.

"I owe him big time. I'm keeping an eye on his wife. She's worried something will happen to her too." Finn's face took on a conspiratorial look. "I was hoping you could help me."

"Sure." Jeff nodded to show he understood.

Finn continued. "You knew this guy. Did business from a fancy office on California Street."

"Sure, I know the name," Jeff recalled. "He traded Shit. Artwork. Jewels, that sort of stuff. He was connected in Chinatown."

"And with the Koreans. Like I said, you knew him."

Jeff's eyes lit up suddenly. "Guy was in here, oh, a couple of months ago. A mucky-muck at one of the tech firms down the Peninsula. He was pissed because his suppliers were going to raise their rates."

"Yeah. So?"

"They're all in Korea. Whoever was moving their shipments was in financial trouble and needed to up their prices."

Finn's eyebrows came together. "You think he was talking about Xanthus?"

"Don't know. You said Korea and it came to mind."

The scowl remained on Finn's face. He looked down at the bar while he considered Jeff's words. He doubted Xanthus could have money problems. Philippe was too careful. Finn decided to get back on track. He saw Jeff waiting for him to continue. "Someone wanted Kassar's money or his business. If I don't find out what happened soon, his wife may be endangered because she inherits Xanthus."

Jeff gave a solemn nod.

"I can't stay in one place long because the cops will hear I'm back and then I'm cooked."

"How can I help?"

"See what you can find out. A lot goes on in this place."

"Sure. How do I reach you?"

"I'll be back."

Jeff smiled. "Okay, Arnooold."

Finn reached for his wallet and his face went flat. "Son of a bitch!"

Jeff looked wary.

"That asshole got my wallet."

"You mean that drunk?" Jeff said. "Don't worry. Emile will know where to find him. We'll get it back."

"Yeah but—" Finn grit his teeth and looked at his friend. "I can't get stopped without ID."

"We'll get it." He added a gesture that took in the bar. "And this one's on me. Get lost. Have a good night."

~

Emma descended the front steps of Forest Hill Muni station into the damp, ominous fog. It blew cold across Laguna Honda Boulevard from the Pacific Ocean two-and-one-half miles to the west. A handful of weary passengers crossed the sidewalk to the bus stop and huddled beneath their turned up collars. Emma veered left at the bottom of the steps and began the seven-minute walk to her home.

She trudged mindlessly down the hill, pleased that she'd stopped at the Brassiere S&P for duck breast because the wine was keeping her warm. At the corner of Plaza, she turned left onto the short, dark side street that brought her to Magellan Avenue. The road traversed sideways around Forest Hill and divided into two lanes. Emma turned right onto the lower lane and headed up the sidewalk. The row of expensive homes on her right were dark because of the late hour. Any light coming from uphill was blocked by eight feet of concrete wall and boxwood hedge abutting the far side of the narrow lane.

She had passed three homes when she heard a loud pulsing sound, the noise an unmuffled car makes when the driver takes his foot off the gas. The racket grew and she guessed the car had rounded the corner onto Plaza. It became throaty and she believed it was accelerating onto Magellan behind her. The hammering grew unbearably loud in the narrow street and sent shivers up her spine: an evil sound approaching. Emma covered her ears with her hands and waited for the vehicle to pass. When it didn't, her anxiety spiked. The car lurked behind her, loud and threatening. She couldn't help looking over her shoulder. A midnight-blue Corvette crept slowly at idle, half a block back, its parking lights glowering like the eyes of a stalking carnivore.

She looked quickly up the sidewalk ahead, could just see the turn onto her street, and broke into a swift walk, too proud, and not sufficiently terrified, to run.

~

Finn's train arrived at the Forest Hill Muni station two minutes after Emma's. He stepped into the cold shroud and turned left onto Laguna Honda Boulevard. Ahead of him, barely visible in the mist, a woman turned onto Plaza. It was late for Emma, after 11:00 pm. But if it was her, he'd catch up before she got home, even at his normal pace.

Finn ignored the unmuffled Corvette as it thundered past him, but when he saw it turn onto Plaza, the harbinger circled again inside his head. He broke into a jog. He heard the 'vette accelerate onto Magellan. He still hadn't reached Plaza. Suddenly, the Corvette went quiet. Finn ran faster.

He rounded the corner onto Plaza. After a half-dozen strides, he turned onto Magellan. He followed the uphill slope, but saw no lights on the narrow road. He ran faster. Coming to a slight curve, he finally glimpsed the 'vette's tail lights turning right at the corner ahead onto Castenada. *He's following her.* He pushed the pace but couldn't gain much speed on the uphill grade.

By the time Finn turned onto Castenada and started down the hill, Emma and the 'vette were hidden around another bend. Finn sprinted. When he reached the bend he saw the Corvette's brake lights. It wasn't moving. To the left, Emma was pushing through the gate to her house. As Finn raced toward them, she ran up the steps and into the foyer, out of sight. Finn flew toward the Corvette, his only thought was to rip the driver out of his seat and beat him into the ground. The 'vette departed slowly and Finn thought he could catch it. He ran harder, stretched forward going downhill, balanced on the edge of falling on his face, determined to catch the fleeing car.

He'd almost caught it when suddenly a red glare lit the pavement in front of him. A second later it became a white blaze. *Backup lights.* Finn reacted with reflexes honed during a hundred thousand years of human survival. He went with his momentum. He planted his next step and vaulted into the air, bringing his knees to his chest just as the 'vette, squealing in reverse, passed under him. He cleared the car's roof and landed on the hood, a grazing contact since they were traveling in opposite directions. It sent his tucked body spinning like a billiard ball. Miraculously, he hit the street on his butt and heels and bounced into a forward somersault. He flung his legs and arms away from his body in order to stop tumbling. He landed flat on his back, felt the pavement grind his flesh, but knew he hadn't broken any bones. He skidded to a stop, his feet pointed downhill, the rumbling monster a dozen yards uphill.

Now face up in a glare of headlights, Finn heard the Corvette shift into first. The tires shrieked and his body reacted again without conscious thought. In one motion, he drove his right arm into the pavement, pushed over onto his left side and propelled his body over the curb, onto the sidewalk. The deadly car swerved to hit him but he had moved too fast. The assassin didn't stop, but roared down the hill and out of sight.

Finn stood and gingerly straightened his back. The adrenaline in his bloodstream suppressed most of the pain from road rash. He walked delicately to Emma's house, trying to prevent his clothes from scraping over his abraded skin. He stopped at the gate and bent at the waist, keeping his back arched. With his hands on his knees he breathed deeply until he felt his heart rate slowed. Then he straightened and walked to Emma's front door. She peeked through a narrow opening as he came up the steps.

"You all right?" he asked. She opened wider and stood in the doorway.

"No. Some jerks just chased me home. Scared the you-know-what out of me."

"Yeah, I saw."

"You saw?" her eyes widened and her pitch rose. "Why didn't you do something?"

"I tried, Emma. I was too far away."

"God damn it, Finn, you're supposed to be Johnny-On-The-Spot."

Finn's temper flared. He'd done his best to catch the son of a bitch. Almost got killed. *Let it go*, he thought. *She's scared*. "It's okay, Emma. You're all right."

"I'm not all right." She glared at him. "What did they want?"

"Someone wanted to scare you."

"Well, they succeeded. Should I call the police?"

"No. I'll deal with it."

Emma stepped through the threshold and took Finn's arm. "Come inside. I don't feel like being alone."

Finn didn't acknowledge her hand on his arm. His back had most of his attention. He knew he should stay with Emma, but he wanted to be with Teb. The quandary must have shown on his face.

"Finn!" Emma exclaimed and withdrew her hand.

"Whoever drove that car left because he'd got what he came for. He won't be back."

"Finn, please. I just don't want to be alone with all that's happened."

He looked away. "I know."

"I'm afraid." Her arms crossed her chest and her fingers clutched her shoulders.

"They just wanted to frighten you, Emma."

"All right, fine." She let her hands drop to her side. "You're going to let me down again?"

The words stung. He hadn't made up his mind. He was testing boundaries. He'd deserted her once before and the humiliation still haunted him. Couldn't make that mistake again. "No, Emma. I'm just trying to tell you you're not in danger. Of course I'll stay with you."

"Promise you will protect me while I sort out this business with Philippe and Xanthus."

"You have my word, Emma."

The anxiety faded from her face. If Finn gave his word, she could feel secure. She moved closer and took his arm. "When did you get here, anyway?"

"This afternoon." He put his free hand over hers and looked into his eyes. "Emma. I swear I won't let anyone hurt you. Philippe would have wanted me to keep you safe."

She squeezed his arm tighter.

"Besides, some son of a bitch just tried to kill me. I can't walk away from that."

FRIDAY

Detective Hedges collected Allegra from her hotel on Seventh Street at exactly 8:30 am. He hoped the day would be uneventful. He watched her slide into the front seat. He liked the way she'd styled her hair with a part off to one the side, but said nothing. He remained silent during the four-block drive to the Hall of Justice on Bryant.

Instead of going to his office in the police department he took her across the street to a cafe. Hedges ordered pastries and espresso. He leaned against a counter, munching on a bear claw and watching Allegra page through a thick file. *Let's see how long before she gets to the money.* He had taken several bites of his bear claw before she glanced over at him.

"You say Mister Kassar is no saint. What he is then?"

Hedges wiped crumbs from his mouth with a napkin. "Kassar ran an investment company called Xanthus. He had a partner, Younger Park, who was murdered two years ago." He pointed with the napkin. "That file in your hands was put together by Detective Costello who investigated that case."

Allegra eyed the pile of paper. "Is a lot of information."

Hedges smiled. He'd read it. Wasn't sure he blamed her for being intimidated. "Let me summarize. Kassar arrived here from Lebanon in the nineties. He was an importer, mostly Asian stuff. Did a lot of business with Chinese."

"Yes, Lebanese are good traders."

Hedges continued. "Kassar went to work for a freight agent, Roscoe Pender. Pender did business with the Korean Community. The US Customs and Border Patrol guys thought he was helping them smuggle technology but they never caught him." He now had Allegra's interest.

"Kassar gave Pender the idea to make short-term loans to Korean importers."

"Ah so." She looked pleased with herself. "Is because the importer need money before his goods arrive?"

"Exactly." *She does have a brain.* "Roscoe loaned money using the value of the shipment as collateral. When the shipment arrived the importer paid off Pender's loan with interest."

"Was good business?"

"Kassar thought so. He offered the same service to Chinese importers."

"One must be careful doing business with Chinese." She frowned.

"He was careful," Hedges said. "Kassar made enough to buyout Pender's share of Xanthus. Then, to get more business from the Chinese, he lowered interest rates. But," here he paused and raised a finger. "If the shipment arrived late and the importer couldn't pay off the loan on time, the interest rate would double or triple."

"No. He can do that?" Her eyes grew wide and almost made him laugh.

"Chinese were not happy. Some refused to pay, so Kassar hired tough guys to collect his money."

"Maybe Chinese kill Mister Kassar?"

"No. Kassar was careful. I don't think his crew ever killed any Chinese."

"Then someone else does not like Mister Kassar." She ran one hand through her hair, flipping the ends.

"Well, Kassar made tons of money. He wanted to be a wheeler-dealer. He moved into a prestigious office with his partner, Younger Park, and they started to invest in high tech."

"Then partner was killed," she said.

"Yes."

"And now Kassar is killed."

"You're up to date."

Allegra raised her eyebrows blew threw her lips.

"Yes," Hedges agreed. "Smells like a rat."

She finished her espresso and spoke quietly into the cup, as if to herself. He barely heard her words, "Maybe they not die for same reason." Then she looked at him and he could tell something was on her mind. "What about wife?"

Disappointment. She'd gone off track. But he covered it with a smile. "Been married about four years. But if you look in that file, you'll see the neighbors complained several times about loud noise and shouting from their home."

"I will read file later." She pushed it aside. "You talk to her?"

"Yes. She seemed quite genuine, she and her brother."

Allegra looked down at her handwritten notes. "The brother is Dan?"

"Yes, an accountant. Not really involved in the business, but helping out his sister now that her husband is deceased." Hedges stuffed the last chunk of bear claw into his mouth.

"I see." Allegra closed her notebook. "You say Mr. Kassar make a lot of money. Such man must have enemies."

Hedges held up a hand until he had finished chewing and swallowed. "Roscoe Pender. Thinks he was cheated when Holliday sold Kassar the business. He is the first loose string we will pull to see how the ball unravels. You and I are going to drop in on him later."

Hedges was surprised to see Allegra's eyes light up like she was excited about meeting him.

"We can see if he is real enemy," she said.

He wiped his fingers with a napkin. "You won't have any trouble understanding his character."

~

Finn had to admit that staying with Emma last night instead of with Teb made him grumpy. Whereas, almost getting run over by a blue Corvette genuinely pissed him off. He found it hard to control his feelings so that he didn't snap at Emma, a problem he solved by speaking very little during the Muni ride from her home to the Embarcadero. She seemed lost in her own thoughts and didn't mind his silence.

They waited by the cafe on the Mezzanine inside 101 California Street. When Dan arrived, he acknowledged Finn but otherwise ignored him. Brother and sister took sixteen-ounce coffees and descended the escalator to the lobby. Finn opted for breakfast. A hostess seated him at a table by the railing and he watched them stroll toward the elevators.

~

Roscoe Pender stood smack in the middle of the atrium at 101 California Street, his eyes studying the flow of pedestrians heading to work. The former basketball player was hard to miss, six-feet-five-inches, wearing a brown leather sports jacket over an orange rayon shirt. He silently complimented himself on his good taste when he saw someone do a double take at his appearance. *Today is the first step*, he told himself, *to getting back what I lost to Philippe Kassar.*

Roscoe saw Emma and Dan emerge from the crowd. He straightened to his full six-five and approached, smiling. Emma saw him before Dan. She looked startled and turned away quickly toward the elevators. *Well shit. If I can't get to the lovely widow, I guess the brother will have to do.* Roscoe had met Dan socially and thought he was a wimp. But maybe he could reach Emma through him. Dan angled to go around Roscoe, but the taller man stayed him with a hand to his arm.

"Dan, a minute."

Dan stopped and looked Roscoe in the eye with no hint of friendliness.

"I'm sorry about Philippe," he began.

"Well thanks, Roscoe." Dan moved to follow Emma, but Roscoe tightened his grip.

"Listen," Roscoe was still smiling. "Since Philippe can no longer run Xanthus, I want your gorgeous sister to consider something."

"What's that?" Dan's tone suggested the answer wouldn't matter. He held his coffee and waited.

"I'm now the only one who knows enough about Xanthus to run it."

Dan shook his head and tried to push past Roscoe.

"You know Xanthus was mine before Philippe stole it?"

Dan stopped and again looked him in the eye.

"So what? You think you're entitled? Besides, I understood he paid plenty for it."

Roscoe opened his mouth to object, but remembered he wasn't here to argue. "All right. Look. It's complicated. The business involves a lot of inter-personal relationships. Business contacts. People overseas. The kind of insider knowledge that takes years to get. A gentle woman like your sister doesn't have any of that. In which case, she shouldn't really want the business. It will drive her crazy. It will fail. She will wind up with nothing."

Dan stepped back.

"I know the business," Roscoe pressed. "Your lovely sister doesn't."

Dan took another step back. "Can't be that hard. If Philippe could do it, she can."

Roscoe displayed his open palms. "Dan, I'm trying to help out here. Why don't you ask her to sell it to me? It's the right thing to do. She'll retire wealthy and you'll both be much happier."

Dan turned toward the elevator. "Not today, Roscoe."

Roscoe raised his voice at Dan's receding figure. "I'll make her a hellava good offer."

Without looking back, Dan shook his head. Roscoe sniffed and cast his eyes about for the nearest exit.

~

From the cafe, Finn watched Dan ascend in one of the glass-fronted elevators and Roscoe walk toward the Davis Street exit. What were they doing? They shared a common interest in Myrna, but Roscoe wouldn't have approached Dan to discuss her. He suppressed a smirk. Certainly not first thing in the morning. More likely Roscoe wanted Xanthus and hoped to get it back now that Philippe was dead. The idea of Roscoe taking over the company didn't appeal to Finn. It certainly wouldn't benefit Emma. He cancelled his breakfast order and left quickly so he could catch up with Dan.

When the elevator door opened at the forty-fifth floor, Finn spotted his man walking toward Xanthus' offices. "Dan!" He saw him stop and turn. "Oh, Hauken. It's you." Finn ignored the disdain in Dan's voice.

Finn closed the distance between them, stopping an arm's length away. The two men looked eye-to-eye. After a moment, Finn cracked a smile.

"Good morning, Dan. Nice to see you again too. You know anyone who drives a blue Corvette?"

"Why?"

"He might know something about Philippe."

"No, I don't know anyone with a blue 'vette."

"What did Roscoe want?"

"Wants to buy Xanthus."

"Still feels like Philippe stole it," Finn smiled. "What'd you tell him?"

"I said, 'No way.' I hate the guy."

"Good for you. He's a real toad."

"Yeah? What's that make you then?" Dan turned around and marched toward the office. Finn watched his back. If only for Emma's sake, he would like to recover the man's respect. When Dan reached the office door, he looked back at Finn like he'd just remembered something. "Oh by the way, the Bureau of Industry and Security called yesterday. I'm sending them your way."

Finn was dumbfounded. "What could I possibly tell them?"

A thin smile appeared on Dan's lips. "It's the Department of Commerce. You'll think of something."

Finn watched him open the door and enter the Xanthus suite. *What's he thinking?*

~

Logan sat at his favorite table in The Emerald Rose. He concentrated on breathing, relaxing, willing away the anxiety while waiting for Roscoe to join him. His problem was that he never knew which Roscoe would show up. The focused athlete that played basketball at Duke University or the sexual predator they expelled for coercing freshman cheerleaders. To say the least, the man was erratic. Roscoe would manage an international business deal one day and lose himself drunk in a titty bar the next. Even when he had both oars in the water, no one knew whether they were on the same side of the boat.

Logan watched the maitre d' escort the former athlete to the table, a big man walking with a flowing but disjointed stride. Logan flashed on the scarecrow from the Wizard of Oz and laughed out loud at the image of Ray Bolger loping toward him in a bright orange shirt, brown suede jacket, and loose camel slacks.

Roscoe stood while the maitre d' pulled the chair away from the table. He gave Logan a puzzled look.

"What? You like this jacket? I just got it. On sale."

Logan grinned. "Thanks for coming, Roscoe. Good to see you."

They ordered brunch. The waiter collected their menus. The busboy poured coffee. After he was out of earshot, Logan sat back in his chair and regarded Roscoe, noticed the deep worry lines in his broad face. "This is some business with Philippe."

Roscoe's eyes lit up. "I was there."

"What?" Logan leaned forward in his seat.

"Holliday sent me to talk to Kassar. Catch him alone, away from everything. He wanted him to lighten up with the Chinese and keep the Koreans happy."

"You didn't kill him?"

"Naw," he scoffed and then caught himself. "I might have. Except that when I found the fat fuck, he was lying on a bed with his guts spilled all over the floor. Jesus, what a disgusting stench."

"What happened?" Logan's upper lip curled.

"Somebody hated him worse than me."

Logan looked into the distance. "Jesus, I wonder—"

"I don't know. But Holliday's worried about what'll happen to Xanthus. It's why you and me got a job to do."

Logan struggled to picture Kassar with a gash across his abdomen.

"Younger once told me he thought Kassar was stealing," Roscoe offered.

Logan looked into his eyes. "Maybe that had something to do with Younger's untimely demise."

"Well, Younger's main worry was the same as Holliday's: Kassar dealt too much with the Chinese. Younger ragged on Kassar constantly for not keeping up the Korean side of the business." Roscoe laughed. "Maybe Kassar just wanted to shut him up."

Logan rolled his eyes.

"How'd it go at Xanthus this morning?"

"I didn't talk to the wife. Just the brother."

"Her brother is running the show?" His pitch rose.

"Not running it. Just helping her out. He's some kind of finance guy."

"Yeah?"

"Who else in San Francisco wears a suit and tie with a button down shirt?"

"You mean he's Ivy League?"

Roscoe nodded. "Anyway, he didn't seem real receptive to me taking over the business."

Logan was sympathetic. "Well, he's not the decision maker. When she hears a number she likes, he won't matter."

Roscoe rubbed his hands together and displayed a salacious grin. "Ah, the lovely wife. I've wanted some of that ass since the first time I saw her."

"Listen," Logan's eyes narrowed. "I know you got a thing for her but don't be a jerk-off."

Roscoe raised his palms. "Kassar's out of the way now and that juicy little twist is just begging for someone like me to come along and ram it in up to her eyeballs."

"Jesus!" Logan cringed. "Haven't you been in enough trouble with your debauchery?"

"Yeah. I got to be careful. But she is choice, man. We're talking prime meat. Better than prime. Super prime." Logan saw his eyes were ablaze. His lips were wet with saliva. "Besides, you know me. I wouldn't do anything stupid."

Logan let the remark hang for a moment. "Roscoe. Stay focused for once . . . or quit playing dumb. I'm not sure which."

Roscoe wiped his mouth and took another sip of coffee. The waiter brought their meal. Neither man spoke while they ate. After a while, Roscoe commented without looking up from his meal. "I saw Finn Hauken at Xanthus."

"You did?"

"Little fucker. Surprised the shit out of me. I thought he'd left for parts unknown."

"He did."

"Then what's he doing back here, especially if the cops want him for Younger's murder?"

"I couldn't say why he's here. But now that your friend Holliday is back, I expect he'll probably take care of that nasty little shit."

"I always thought Hauken was fay."

Logan gave him a condescending smile. "Oh yeah?"

"Well, they say he never killed anyone and he was a circus clown for Christ's sake. They're all faggots."

"I wouldn't let him hear you say that."

Roscoe's look said, *get real.* Logan shrugged it off but added, "Don't kid yourself. Kassar was probably the only guy who could take Hauken one-on-one."

"Yeah. I give it to Kassar. He was something else. He got in my face once. Bad freakin' news."

"Kassar thought Hauken was a stand-up guy. Never took more than an eye for an eye." Logan paused. "Not exactly your way, is it?"

Roscoe started to object but the busboy arrived to clear the table. Logan threw a credit card into the bill in the silver tray. They waited until they were alone.

"Don't worry about Hauken," Logan continued. "Just keep on Emma to sell. Consider it your chance to steal Xanthus back."

The waiter returned Logan's card and said, "Your driver is here, sir."

The two men stood and shook hands. "Thanks, Logan. Hey, when you get to the car, remind that asshole, Dwight, he owes me money."

Logan nodded, but had no intention of fulfilling the request.

~

Finn departed the KT high-speed rail line at Evans and Third and reminded himself to be nice no matter what happened. He walked under the noonday sun toward R&P Tool & Die. Roscoe might be an idiot, but Philippe had insisted Finn lay off him. He would do his best to honor his late mentor's wishes.

Ten feet before Finn reached the entrance to R&P, Roscoe came out of the Quonset. He turned away and walked to the mailbox. He stood sorting mail while Finn came up behind him with a big grin on his face.

"Roscoe Pender, as I live and breathe."

Roscoe jumped higher than Finn would have guessed possible and came down facing him, his mouth open and his eyes bulging.

"Geez, you trying to scare me or what? Sneaking up like that."

"You nervous about something, Roscoe?"

"I was fine until a few seconds ago. What do you want?"

Finn continued to smile. "Saw you and Dan this morning."

"Yeah. I saw you, too. I didn't think you noticed me."

"You're too big to miss, Roscoe." Finn laughed.

"Is that so? Well, for a hot shit you sure ain't much to look at."

Finn ignored the jibe. "So what's up with you and Dan?"

"I'm going to buy Xanthus, is what."

"Buy it?" Finn raised his eyebrows, which caused Roscoe to frown.

"You trying to be funny?"

Finn gave him a dumb smile.

Roscoe seemed to relax. "Hey, I got no beef with them. But now Philippe's gone and they can't make Xanthus work. I can."

"Buy it?" Finn said again and cocked his head. It was way too easy to yank Roscoe's chain.

"Aw cut it out, will ya'. Let bygones be bygones. I got cash. I'm gonna make them a good offer."

"Yeah?"

"That's right. And what do you care anyway? You're not even around here anymore."

The front door of the building opened and two solid-looking men in blue coveralls stepped onto the sidewalk. Finn saw them and guessed they had expected Roscoe to return sooner when he caught Roscoe nodding to show he was okay. Finn returned his gaze to Roscoe

"Just keeping an eye on things," he said and waited until recognition dawned. Then Roscoe's eyes grew dark and his lips curled.

"Ah. The pretty widow. I forgot you two had a thing before Philippe."

Finn held the dumb, smile but Roscoe knew he'd touched a nerve.

"What? You don't like the idea of me running my tongue down around that belly, between them sweet lips, inside that tight little asshole?"

Finn did his best not to react.

"Don't worry, Ace," Roscoe played innocent, but not well. "This is strictly for cash. And I'm in it for the money. You got that?"

"Just checking," Finn kept the smile, but caution lights flashed in his head. He changed the subject. "Still with Myrna?"

Roscoe scoffed. "That bitch? I have no idea whose dick she's sucking these days."

Finn chuckled. "Roscoe, you always were such a caring person."

"That all you wanted, Hauken?"

"Unless you know someone who drives a blue Corvette."

Roscoe's eyes bored into him. Finn saw the two workman shift their feet like they were preparing to move. He readied himself, hoping they would.

"What's the deal?" Roscoe said after a few moments.

Finn met Roscoe's stare. "I want to meet the driver."

"A blue 'vette, huh? Probably a standup guy."

"So? You know?"

"Fuck you, Hauk."

Finn felt his heart rate soar. Philippe's warnings blared in his head. He stared hard at Roscoe, then realized what he was about to do. He relaxed his fists, took a step back. "Another time, Roscoe."

"Not likely," Roscoe snarled. The boys in blue laughed. Roscoe laughed with them. Finn walked away.

~

Detective Hedges watched Allegra across his desk study her notes over the remains of their lunch. Her boss had sent her alone to deal with the Americans. In the last twenty-four hours, the pretty blond attorney had piqued his interest. She had a lively way about her, alert, full of spunk and curiosity. She wore stylish shoes and tailored clothes. Hedges caught himself before he plunged any further into fantasy.

She raised her eyes from the notes and looked at him with a puzzled expression. "It says here Holliday Park was from Russia. But his name is Korean."

"He is Korean. His grandfather is chairman Park Seung-Rok of RTE, one of Korea's big conglomerates. Among other things, it operates ocean freight terminals and his parents lived and worked in Vladivostok. Where he was born. He has dual citizenship in those countries."

"Why nationality is important?"

Hedges thought for a moment. "Holliday came to Silicon Valley to get into high tech. He had plenty of money. But he was and is a foreign national. He needed an American partner in order to work with certain technologies. He funded Xanthus, made Roscoe the American owner, and made his brother, Younger Park, a partner."

"Younger Park was equal partner?"

"Not sure," Hedges reflected. "Anyway, when Younger was murdered, Detective Costello arrested a suspect, but the man escaped."

"Kassar was not suspect?" Her eyes widened.

"I don't think so."

Allegra scowled at him. "If Park have more money, Kassar should be suspect."

"I'm sure Costello thought of that."

The answer didn't appear to satisfy Allegra, Hedges noted. She slumped in her chair. But not for long. "So, Mister Kassar go to Chianti on vacation. He dine with two men, *teppisti*, we say in Italy. Here, you say hoodlum. Next morning he is find stabbed. Chief Inspector Romero say mobile phone and jewelry are gone." She looked at him hard. "Why we care about Koreans and Russians? Why we don't look for phone and jewels? I want to meet this Roscoe Pender."

Hedges was speechless.

~

"The inspector sent his assistant, the lawyer, to help solve the murder," Nico told his partner. The two men shared a table in the Piazza del Campo. They dined comfortably in the twilight, despite the stifling summer heat in Siena.

"To America?" Alfonse asked over the huge steak Florentine on the table between them. "Your cousin told you this?"

Nico nodded. A passing waiter sloshed mineral water into their glasses and hurried away.

"What do you think?" Alphonse sipped his wine. He was short, dark, and serious. The opposite of Nico, who was gregarious, corpulent, and connected.

"If the lawyer is successful, it will be hard for us," Nico said.

"I agree. What should we do?"

"We will make the trip. Sever the connection."

"To America?" Alfonse lowered his wine glass.

"Yes." Nico glanced at him.

"You're joking." Alfonse leaned forward. "We cannot eliminate a problem in America as we do in Italy."

"We will take care of the woman and be gone before they know we were there."

Alfonse thought for a moment. His friend's judgment had never been wrong before. "When do we go?"

"In the morning."

~

Logan returned from lunch, hung his suit coat on a hanger in the closet of his office and sat down at his desk to face a depressing stack of documents. The more he searched among them, the more morose he became. He simply could not find a solution for his money problems. After a while, he leaned back in his chair, turned away from the desk and stared out the window. From his Jackson Street office he gazed at the Transamerica pyramid. But it only made his head feel heavy. That monstrous symbol of wealth. It was an icon of gloom. He sunk down in his chair.

Logan heard the creak of leather behind him. Someone had taken a seat on the other side of the desk. The owner of GP Investments turned, ready to complain about the interruption, but stopped when he didn't recognize the intruder.

The visitor couldn't have been thirty. He wore an expensive sports jacket with an open shirt. His longish brown hair framed a face with the dumbest smile Logan had ever seen. But he looked familiar.

"Do I know you?" The eyes, no the smile, started to ring a bell.

"It's been a while." The voice did it. The consternation left Logan's face.

"Hauken. You look different."

"I've been away." Finn leaned back in the chair.

"You here because of Philippe?"

Finn nodded. "I owe him."

"Too bad about him." Logan sounded like he didn't give a rat.

"Thought you might know what happened." Finn kept looking at him. His smile didn't change.

"Why would I?" Logan started to feel uncomfortable.

"You got an interest." Finn's smile brightened. "You are Xanthus' largest shareholder after Philippe."

Logan was caught off guard, but hid it well. "Yeah, well, it's not an especially desirable holding these days." He shuffled the papers on his desk.

"So you did something about it?"

Logan shook his head. "Please. That's not me. And anyway, I don't even know what happened."

"He was stabbed." Finn no longer smiled. "Cops think it was a robbery."

"Why? Something missing?"

"His jewelry and his phone."

Logan caught his breath when he heard that Kassar's smartphone was missing. *Why didn't Roscoe tell me?* He tried to keep his face relaxed, realized he wanted the intruder gone. "What do you want, Hauken?"

"Just trying to make sure no one else gets hurt."

"That's a switch. I thought your job was hurting people."

Finn ignored it. "You know anyone who drives a blue Corvette?"

"No." Logan twisted in his seat. "And I don't know where you're going with this, but I've got work to do. Now, would you please leave?"

"I thought you could tell me why someone might want Philippe dead."

Logan shook his head. "Goodbye Hauken."

"As things stand, you've got the largest interest in Xanthus."

"Hauken. That's enough." But Logan glimpsed an image of Holliday Park saying almost the same thing to him earlier.

"That is, aside from Emma." Finn continued and Logan saw his eyes glowing with emotion. "Someone's threatening her." Finn cocked his head. "That wouldn't be you, would it, Logan?"

Those stories of Hauken's brutality. Logan felt his hands shaking. "I don't know anything about Emma being threatened." He needed to steady his voice. "If I had an interest in acquiring the rest of Xanthus, it would be strictly business. You understand? Nothing personal in any way."

The door to Logan's office opened. Dwight, the driver-bodyguard, crossed the room and stood behind Finn.

"This is Dwight, Hauken. He'll see you out." Logan looked at the bodyguard. "Careful, Dwight. Circus acrobats can be tricky."

Finn stood and faced the scowling Dwight.

"Is that what you were, an ac-ro-bat?" Dwight stressed the syllables, sneering as he reached his right hand across Finn's body to take his right arm. Finn grabbed the extended hand with his left and twisted outward. The wrist bent back on itself and forced Dwight to his knees. He sank with a low groan. Finn applied sufficient pressure to keep him in pain and unable to move. He looked back at Logan who was now standing behind his desk with his mouth open.

"Thanks, Logan. I'll find my own way out."

Logan closed his mouth and watched Finn release Dwight, then step around him to the door.

"Hauken!" he almost shouted. Finn turned. "Be careful. For your own sake." His lips drew a thin smile. "No more Philippe, no more protection." Finn's expression didn't change. He walked out of the office.

The bodyguard stood and cradled his right arm. Logan saw the humiliation on his face. "Okay, Dwight. Don't worry about it. He won't be around long."

Dwight left. Logan dropped back into his chair, pursed his lips and exhaled a loud sigh. *Roscoe, that idiot. I've got enough problems.*

~

Dan didn't like breaking bad news. Especially to his sister. He'd spent a long night deep in the company's books and didn't like what he'd found. But he had no choice. It was his sister, after all. He followed Emma down a corridor on the forty-fifth floor of 101 California. When they reached Philippe's office, he held the door. Inside, Dan dropped the folder he was carrying on Philippe's desk and took a chair by the coffee table. After parking her briefcase beside the desk, Emma approached the credenza, saw the Nespresso machine was on, and opened a box of capsules.

"You want coffee?"

"A double, please."

He watched her across the desk drop a capsule in the machine, then look back over her shoulder at him.

"Roscoe wants the business. What should we do about it?"

"He still believes Philippe ripped him off."

"Roscoe was afraid of Philippe. Did I ever tell you about the time Philippe caught him trying to hit on me?" She chuckled. "Told him if he came around again he'd bite off his testicles."

Dan's shoulders shook from a silent laugh. "Philippe was a bull."

"He was." She placed a coffee in front of him and sat in Philippe's chair with her own. "I like that Roscoe wants to buy Xanthus. Only question is whether he has the money."

"The only question is whether he will believe you screwed him when he buys Xanthus and discovers it's broke." He reached for his coffee.

"What do you mean?"

Dan pointed at the folder on the desk. "I dug through the books you gave me. I couldn't believe it. I found expenses allocated to projects that didn't exist. That money's already spent. Then I found receivables booked in the future but already collected. You have no money coming in. If I saw it, the bank, the shareholders, regulators—they will, too."

"Everything's gone?" She sat upright.

"You're broke."

"That son of a bitch."

"You didn't know?"

"No."

"Philippe kept it from you?"

"Yes, God damn it."

Dan lowered his eyes. "I'm sorry, Emma. I thought you were close."

She slammed the desk with the side of her clenched fist. "We were close." Dan saw tears welling in her eyes. "Now, he's dead and no one knows where the money went."

"Oh, an amount that large? It'll turn up," Dan looked up from his coffee.

"How large? You don't mean all 40 million?"

"Yes. The value of the entire company."

Her mouth hung open for a second. "I don't believe it. Who else knows?"

"I don't think he told anyone. You didn't know."

"And there's nothing we can do?"

"Not about the money. Obviously, you don't know where Philippe stashed it. But there's Roscoe. If you can figure out a way for him to buy Xanthus and not believe you ripped him off . . . "

Dan watched Emma look into her coffee cup for several moments. When she raised her eyes to him again, her mouth curled up like she'd licked a toad. "He's a prick, but a stupid one."

~

Holliday Park was hunting men. One man, to be precise: Finn Hauken. Patience and money had finally paid off. A spy saw him after almost two years. Last night. At a bar he'd just passed on Sixteenth Street. Holliday had checked. Hauken wasn't there now, but he could be anywhere in the neighborhood. Holliday drove and searched. His only distraction was the vehicle.

"I hate this piece of *govno*!" he shouted. No one heard him from inside the Sprinter, poking along Sixteenth Street, the steering wheel wet with sweat. The tall and narrow van felt like it would tip over if he turned the wheel a hair too much.

The mid afternoon sun had warmed the interior and Holliday rolled down the window when he was a block from the BART station at Mission Street. He steered past a taqueria, eyeing the oncoming pedestrians on his right. A man talking on a phone caught his attention. He felt his mouth gape open. The man's features seemed to fall into place one by one until Holliday recognized Finn Hauken. He saw his prey pocket the phone and look back at him. Holliday felt his stomach tighten and his heart rate soar. *Ohooiet!* "Holy Fuck!" He repeated in English.

In an instant, he forgot his fear of the van. No oncoming traffic. Holliday spun the steering wheel left as far as it would go. The Sprinter swerved across the oncoming lane and bounced onto the opposite curb. Didn't tip over. He jammed the brakes. Threw the shift into reverse. Tires squealed. The van lurched backward into the curb behind. Anxiety rippled through Holliday. *Don't let him get away!* He looked back and saw Hauken staring at him. Never mind. Another shift and he trounced the accelerator. More squeals.

But Hauken was nowhere in sight. He must have ducked down the alley on the left. Holliday entered the turn way too fast. He couldn't control the Sprinter. It screeched, slid into a parked Ford with a tremendous bang, and came to a stop. Holliday shoved the shift into reverse and floored the accelerator. It lurched backward. Without taking his foot off the gas he jammed the shift into drive. There was a loud bang and a jerk that snapped his head back.

Another yowl of tires and he shot down the alley. There. Hauken sprinting ahead, looking quickly to both sides. Holliday saw a house blocking the end of the street. They'd turned into a blind alley. He stepped harder on the gas. Avoided hitting the cars parked on both sides of the street. He grinned. No exit. Hauken was trapped.

Just when Holliday felt like he could reach out and grab Hauken's heels, the man suddenly juked right and bounded over the sidewalk. His hands caught the galvanized rail at the top of an eight-foot chain-link fence topped with rolls of barbed wire. One toe lodged in the chain links while the other leg hung free.

Holliday flung the wheel to the right, to catch him. He didn't see the three-foot-tall stanchion embedded in the sidewalk. The front of the van swallowed the pole. Suddenly, Holliday couldn't see. The airbag exploded in his face. His chest slammed into the seatbelt. For a second, he didn't know where he was. He felt deep pain across his chest.

Holliday slapped the airbag out of his face. Hauken hung on the fence in front of him. He must have paused when he heard the Sprinter crash. But now he donkey-kicked his free leg up and over his head, pushed off the fence with the other foot, and levered himself into a handstand on the top rail. At the apex, he released one hand, pirouetted 180 degrees and grabbed the top rail again with his free hand. Holliday froze, his mouth open, awed by the spectacle. Hauken's momentum carried him over the fence, but not over the barbed wire. At the last possible moment, he bent his knees, kicked his legs straight and pushed off with both arms, just clearing the razor sharp coils. He landed in the empty yard on his feet, facing Holliday. Didn't pause, but spun around. Holliday watched him disappear into a narrow walkway beside the house. He closed his mouth and tried to swallow, but his throat was too dry.

Apart from the pain in his chest, Holliday felt okay. He couldn't open the driver's door but the rear doors were undamaged. He exited and left the no-good van where it was, its hood mashed around a stanchion, oil, water, and antifreeze running over the sidewalk.

He cursed himself in Korean as he walked up the alley back to Sixteenth Street. He'd lost control of himself the moment he saw Hauken on the sidewalk. His performance had been disgusting. Pounding heart. Shaking hands. Unskilled driving. An overanxious rookie mistake. Surprise had made him forget all of his training. The sudden shock of seeing a chance to avenge his brother had overwhelmed him. Holliday scolded himself for amateurish behavior until he reached Sixteenth street. By then, his thoughts had calmed and framed a more positive message There would be no repeat of this foolishness. Next time, he would be prepared.

~

Out on Valencia, Finn calmed himself. Emma had told him that Holliday was gone. Yet he had just tried to run him down in the Sprinter. *How had the Korean found me so fast?*

He walked toward Sixteenth Street, breathing slowly, reviewing his mental mug shots for other people that wanted to hurt him. Ahead, a group of provocatively dressed Hispanic girls walked toward him. The figure of one girl in particular caught his fancy and, in spite of himself, his eyes followed her as she passed. He glanced over his shoulder to see if the rear view was as inspiring as the front.

The alluring image of her figure hovered in his mind as he turned forward, but vanished in an instant when he found himself staring at a blue uniform inches from his face.

The cop placed his hands on Finn's shoulders to prevent a collision and keep them both from falling.

"Hey, take a breather there, fella."

He stiffened at the touch. Just for a second, but enough for the cop to feel it. Finn felt his shoulders gripped in hands with measured force. He had to relax. He looked away.

"Hold on a minute," the cop said. Finn didn't look at him. "You okay?"

"You startled me, that's all." He was calm now. He managed a small grin and looked directly at the cop. The officer studied him with a look of indecision. It wasn't turning into the kind of day Finn wanted.

"Maybe you'd better show me some ID."

Finn delivered the stupid grin. "I think my wallet is at the Panama Hotel."

"Oh, that's the best one I've hear today." The cop's face went from indecisive to all business and Finn saw he needed to dial up the charm.

"I was in there last night." He smiled in earnest. "I'm on my way to see the bartender now. Get it back."

The cop looked him over for a moment and then relaxed his grip, but not his vigilance. "Since we're practically there, how about we drop in together?"

"Sure thing, officer," Finn kept the smile.

The cop kept one hand on Finn's arm and gave it a shake. "Can I depend on you?"

"Like a faithful dog."

The policeman turned Finn around and steered him toward the police station kitty-corner from where they stood. Finn didn't like it.

"Hey, I thought we were going to the Panama Hotel?"

"Relax," the cop released Finn's arm. "I have to get something, then we're on our way."

A collection of lackluster faces greeted Finn from the benches lining the passage walls in the station foyer. A metal scanner poised at the far end, a barrier to anyone who desired further entry. The cop gestured for Finn to take a seat. "I'll be two minutes."

Finn found a vacancy and sat. He realized he was sweating. The cop disappeared around the scanner. Finn stared into space and weighed whether to leave or stay. He heard the main door open and looked over. The boyish detective from the airport and the attractive blond woman entered the foyer. She saw him in the same instant and their eyes locked. Puzzlement crossed her face and her pace slowed. The detective followed her glance and immediately recognized Finn from the airport.

"Hello, hot shot," he boomed in an incongruous bass voice. "Something we can do for you?"

Finn reluctantly shifted his eyes from Allegra to Hedges.

"No thanks. Someone's already helping me. I'm just waiting for him."

Hedges laughed and looked at Allegra "Look at that. Here one day and already he's in trouble."

Allegra's eyes never left Finn. "Maybe is not trouble why he is here."

Hedges smiled and shook his head. "C'mon, Avvocatessa. Detective Costello is waiting for us."

Allegra continued to look at Finn as she and Hedges walked past the scanner.

~

Jeff reached beneath the bar, retrieved a wallet and dropped it on the surface in front of him.

"Yeah, we got it," he said looking over the bar at Finn standing beside a cop. "The idiot tried to pass your ID here," he turned a disbelieving glance at the cop. "In the same bar where he swiped it. Does that make the top-ten list of dumbest criminals or what?"

The policeman picked up the wallet, removed the driver's license and studied it. "Andrew Hauken. I seem to recall that name from somewhere." He turned over the license, saw the back was blank, and turned it back over. "You know this guy?" He cocked his head toward Finn.

Finn kept his eyes steady on Jeff.

"Sure," Jeff looked at cop. "Regular customer. I'll vouch for him if he agrees to stop tap dancing on the bar when he gets drunk." Finn looked away and rolled his eyes. The cop eyed Jeff.

"He really do that?" His tone suggested he didn't care one way or the other.

"And worse," Jeff said. "You want to hear more?"

The policeman dropped the license and wallet on the bar. "No thanks. That's enough for one day." He turned for the door and scowled at Finn. "If I suddenly remember how I heard your name, I'll be back."

Once the door had closed behind the cop, Jeff stared at Finn with consternation. "Christ, man. What was that all about?"

Finn collapsed onto a barstool and let his anger roll. "Shit." He slapped the bar and clenched his jaw. "I can't believe I was that careless." He looked at Jeff. "Thought I was toast."

"You? I damn near soiled my drawers when you walked in with a cop."

"It's not the half of it," Finn shook his head. "That freaking pickpocket told somebody I was back and an enemy just tried to run me over."

"No shit!" Jeff rose up on his toes. "It probably wasn't the slimy pickpocket. I've seen him before. More likely that Korean guy with him."

Finn's eyes flared. "It was definitely the Korean." He held one hand out at arm's length. It shook noticeably, whether from the chase in the ally or the encounter in the police station, Finn couldn't tell. Jeff turned to the backbar and grabbed a bottle from the top shelf. He set a glass in front of Finn and filled it.

"I didn't think anyone would remember me after two years," Finn said.

"You're not exactly forgettable."

Finn sipped the drink. "Yeah, well. Watch me now."

~

Hedges braked the Crown Victoria to a stop two doors away from the Emerald Rose. Parking wasn't permitted on Sutter during evening commute, except for a police cruiser. He shifted into park and turned to Allegra sitting in the passenger seat. "That's it," he said, pointing past her to the restaurant.

Her eyes followed his direction. "Is nice place." She sounded surprised.

"Except for the clientele," Hedges said. He opened his door, walked around the car and held open the passenger door for Allegra. She took his hand and stood. The gesture was completely neutral, but Hedges had seen that she appreciated his consideration. She stood beside him, arranged the sheaf of papers she carried, and nodded to say she was ready.

They walked to the striped red and green awning that extended from the restaurant to the curb. Hedges assumed the lawyer was a rookie. A sudden desire swelled inside him to protect her even though he expected no trouble from Roscoe Pender.

"Nobody saw Roscoe during the days before Kassar was killed," he said as they came to the door.

Allegra gestured with the papers in her hand, "Maybe your suspicion is correct. Maybe we meet real enemy." She stuffed the paper into her purse.

~

Roscoe sat at a table along the back wall, one hand around a cocktail glass before him and the other pressing a phone to his ear.

"She wants fifty million," he announced into the phone and looked up at the waiter approaching with his meal.

Roscoe laughed into the phone. "That's what I said. Give her a couple of days to settle that beautiful ass down." The waiter set the dishes in front of Roscoe, bowed, and backed away. Roscoe nodded and at the same time saw Hedges and a blond woman enter the restaurant and scan the patrons. "Oh shit," he told his caller. "Cops. I gotta go."

Before the detectives spotted him, Roscoe eased his chair back, closed his phone, and ducked through the swinging doors into the kitchen. He wasn't quite fast enough.

~

Hedges saw the kitchen doors shut and quickened his pace, weaving between the surprised diners. Allegra followed him through the swinging doors. Their quarry was almost to the back door of the restaurant by the time Hedges grabbed the back of his jacket.

"Where do you think you're going, Roscoe?" He pulled him to a halt.

Roscoe turned and looked down at the shorter man. "I thought you were trying to return my wife." He pointed to Allegra. "Looks just like her."

"Bullshit, Roscoe. You don't even have a wife."

Roscoe laughed. Hedges released his grip. They stood beside one of the kitchen's stainless steel tables. Hedges made a give-it-to-me gesture and Roscoe emptied his pockets onto the table. Allegra immediately dove into the belongings while Roscoe towered over them, a picture of innocence.

"Kassar's dead," Hedges said. "I assume you heard."

"No hair off my balls," Roscoe's face betrayed nothing. His voice was almost as deep as Hedges'.

"You two didn't exactly get along." Hedges smiled.

"Not true," Roscoe protested. "He worked for me over two years. We got on fine."

"Until he stole your business."

"No. What gave you that idea?"

Hedges gave him a look that said, *Give me a break.*

"I'm serious," Roscoe insisted. "He was a stand-up guy."

"Where were you last Thursday?"

"What?"

"Night Philippe was murdered." Hedges' bass voice resonated through the kitchen. "Nobody saw you during the entire week."

"What? No, I was here. Ask Logan Evans."

Hedges frowned. He backed away and reached into his jacket pocket. "Don't stray. If Logan doesn't alibi you, you're coming with us." He turned to Allegra. "Keep an eye on him while I make the call."

Hedges took out his phone and moved away down the stainless counter.

~

Roscoe watched Allegra leaf through his passport. "Tell me, sweetheart, how well do you know the detective?" He was shooting for charming.

"Not so much. I just arrive from Italy." She didn't look up.

"Maybe you should let me show you around." He grinned.

"Me? No, too much work."

"I know all the best places and the best people." He gave her his best smile and laid a giant hand gently on her shoulder.

Allegra didn't move away. She put the wallet on the countertop, looked Roscoe up and down, and then glared at him with unequivocal contempt. "You are not my type."

The lights clicked off in Roscoe's eyes and his balls sucked up into his abdomen. He snatched his hand from her shoulder. Then looked down the counter where Hedges had just closed his phone and was moving toward them. Allegra held up his passport. "No Italia stamps in passport."

"Yeah? Well, his alibi checks." Hedges gave a heavy sigh. He looked up at him.

"Sorry for the interruption. You may return to your dinner."

Roscoe gloated. He swept his things from the steel table into his huge open hand. He gave Allegra a sharp sneer and strutted through the swinging doors into the dining room to his table.

He watched Hedges follow Allegra to the front door and open it for her.

~

"Well that wasn't what I expected." Hedges grumbled as they walked under the awning toward the car. She must have heard the disappointment in his voice. She looked back over her shoulder at him.

"Maybe was someone else travel to Chianti."

He shook his head. "I had no clue that Logan would be his alibi for the day Kassar was killed. They must have hooked up very recently."

"Who is Logan?" She slowed so he could catch up.

"Another guy with a lot of money who makes more money by taking it from other wealthy people."

"He take money from Mister Kassar?"

Hedges stopped and then Allegra stopped and looked at him. He regarded her with newfound appreciation. "Now that's a question, isn't it? Two shrewd operators. Be tough to pick a victor, but I'd give Kassar the edge."

"What if Logan and Roscoe want takeover of Xanthus? Maybe they hire someone in Siena to kill Mister Kassar."

Hedges scowled. "It's about money, Avvocatessa. Not power."

He saw her jaw tighten and she looked away.

"Mister Kassar take money from Logan. Logan and Roscoe kill him."

"Kill him for money, yes. For revenge, no. Our priorities are different in this country." She resumed her journey to the car, her heels a forceful echo on the pavement.

~

One glance at Myrna told Finn she was trouble. Her animal attraction was so intense and involuntary that it turned lesser men into pigs.

He was on his way to the elevators in 101 California Street when he spotted her through the smoked glass window, on a barstool in the lobby's oak and chrome oasis. A hideaway that was skillfully designed with indirect lighting to flatter the after-work crowd and created a sultry atmosphere to encourage liberal abuse of their corporate credit cards.

The lady had a storied past and a volatile temper, he recalled. Now with Dan, Emma had mentioned. At one time with Philippe, another with Roscoe, and earlier with other men of influence Finn had known in the shady world where his boss had mingled. Finn ranked far below her income threshold, but on occasion, he'd seen a spark in her eyes when they crossed paths. Or maybe it was just a predatory gleam. She was probably waiting for Dan, but she served as an opportunity to get a new take on Philippe's death.

He walked noiselessly through the lounge to an empty barstool beside where she sat, facing away, analyzing an attractive couple down the bar.

"What do you know?" he said with quiet charm. "Philippe's ex. How goes it?"

She swiveled the barstool 10 degrees, enough to indicate she'd heard, not enough to show interest. "Well and truly over him. Especially now he's dead."

"Yeah? And no Dan, either. Maybe we should take advantage."

She nudged the stool another 80 degrees so she could study him in the giant mirror behind the back bar. After a short preview, she turned her head slowly and appraised him with a mixture of interest and skepticism. "Dan's not your biggest fan."

"That settles it then. Another drink?" Finn didn't wait for a reply, but slid onto the barstool and motioned to the bartender.

"What are you doing here, anyway?" her voice dripped with disdain. "I thought you'd found greener pastures."

Finn turned to Myrna. "I missed my friends."

"You got friends?"

A bartender delivered their drinks. Finn took his glass and raised it to Myrna. She tipped hers tentatively in his direction.

"Man buys a drink, he's . . ." She arched an eyebrow at Finn.

"Girl accepts a drink, she's . . ." There was a second or two of silence and then they laughed together, the ice broken.

"People say you're strange." She regarded him now with amusement.

"Like your buddy, Roscoe?" He smiled. "I saw him this morning."

She turned aside and curled her lip. "Another waste of carcass."

"I thought he paid your bills," Finn looked at her in the mirror.

Contempt clouded Myrna's face. "Yeah, well . . ." She sipped her drink. "He hated Philippe."

"Not like he didn't have reason."

"Thought he was a clueless butt plug."

"What?" Finn turned to face her. "Philippe made a pile with Xanthus."

"Strictly luck."

"Nu-uh." Finn shook his head. "I know smart."

"You know his wife, too. Was that smart?"

"Love." Finn gave her a wistful look in the mirror.

"Oh boy. What you don't know about women."

After a pause, Finn said, "What's this got to do with us?"

"Nothing. I thought you wanted to know about Roscoe."

"Not really."

"You know he's fronting for Logan?" She couldn't resist gossiping.

Finn eyebrows shot up. "I thought they didn't get along."

"Logan's broke," she smiled at Finn. "He needs Roscoe even if he is an evil prick."

He grinned. "Roscoe? An evil prick? Why do you say that?"

"You ever hear him talk about Philippe's wife?"

Now he frowned.

"He tried to hit on her once. She told him to shove it. Then told Philippe. Philippe threatened to mail Roscoe's package back to Mama.

Finn flashed her a quick look.

"I can't believe she never told you about that."

He stared into his glass. "She never did." He hadn't considered the possibility that Roscoe was stalking Emma. Nor that he was connected with Logan, who must be backing Roscoe's bid for Xanthus. He felt his jaw tighten. One hand grabbed a cocktail napkin from the bar and crumpled it in his palm. He cursed himself for not putting this together before he saw Logan. An opportunity squandered.

Finn looked over at Myrna and recognized the predatory gleam. She moved forward on the barstool. Her short skirt slid up her thighs. Finn couldn't help but glance down and realized in an instant that he was looking at her artfully sculpted pubic hair.

"Sooo . . . what now?" she taunted.

This would be stupid. That is, unless you forgot dangerous. He brought his eyes back to her face. "I'd love to . . ." he let his voice trail off.

"What?" he saw her body tense. "You shy with girls? Roscoe always said you were—"

"Nothing personal."

"I know some nice boys." Her face filled with mock sincerity. Finn gave a dismissive smile.

"Well, what then?"

"It's complicated."

Myrna sat upright. Her cobalt eyes turned glacial and her voice uncoiled like a serpent.

"Guilt? A woman in your past?"

Finn screwed up his face like he wanted to speak.

"Don't," she spat. "I know all about it."

He did his best to look hurt.

Myrna stood, adjusted her skirt, shoulders, handbag. Then she leaned close to Finn. "Thanks anyway for the beguiling interlude, Finn. I just love twisting on the hook." She tapped his temple with her forefinger and said, with all the sarcasm she could muster, "Tell that brain to let some blood into your shriveled dick before it falls off and someone stomps it."

The air seemed to swirl around Finn as she left, bumping him hard enough that he almost fell off his stool. It felt like a speeding semi had blasted by. He righted himself on the seat. Picked up his glass. Put his elbows on the bar. *Things aren't going well*, he thought. Emma was pissed because he wanted to leave her alone. His sworn enemy had tried to run him over. Twice. He hadn't managed very well with Myrna. Between them, Roscoe and Logan had added nothing to explain what happened to Philippe. *I'm wasting my time.*

Then he thought again. Myrna had just told him that Logan was behind Roscoe's bid for Xanthus. Logan wanted Xanthus. But, knowing him, he wouldn't pay the full price. So he sent Roscoe in to lowball Emma. Finn had never liked Roscoe and now he didn't like Logan. Maybe Logan arranged Philippe's death to get his hands on Xanthus. But he could have just bought Philippe out. *There's something I'm not seeing.*

SATURDAY

That blond-haired bitch, Roscoe hadn't thought of anything else since the Emerald Rose. Occasionally he got as far as, *Her and that smart-ass little shit detective.* But his rancor swelled to its peak whenever he saw the image of her eyes filled with complete and final rejection. Yet, he couldn't get her out of his mind. *God damn, she had nice tits. What the fuck was wrong with her? Sick bitch.*

He lit another cigarette and cracked the driver's window of the Corvette. From his vantage in the alley he could see into several of the houses around him though he doubted the inhabitants could see him through the 'vette's tinted side windows. Through the windshield, the morning sun backlit the Kassar home. The rear of the house appeared in shadow except for Emma's large bedroom. Sunlight reflecting off a window on the house next door shined into it like a searchlight.

Lucky surprise. Roscoe watched Emma rise from the bed and stand before the window. She dropped her nightgown to let sunlight warm her naked body and stretched her arms above her head. Roscoe couldn't believe his good fortune. He held the cigarette in one hand and with the other reached down, undid his belt and his fly, arranged himself, and began to masturbate. He watched her stretch and pose in the spotlight, oblivious to his lustful homage. Roscoe, on the other hand, the one that mattered, was in total concentration on Emma,moving like he'd never imagined. His eyes began to glaze.

"You . . . bitch . . ." Tension in his crotch signaled his forthcoming crescendo. Roscoe hadn't really prepared for what was to come and glanced around for a receptacle. He balanced the cigarette on the dash above the speedometer, grabbed a used coffee cup from the seat next to him, and moved it into position just in time.

He closed his eyes and felt the overwhelming, joyful release. Sublime pulses shot through his groin. He moaned and threw his head back. A split second later glorious ecstasy turned to burning pain.

"Ow! Shit!" he looked down, saw a glowing spark. "What the fuck?"

The lit cigarette had rolled off the dash onto Roscoe's exposed genitals. He snapped the door handle. The door flew open. His hands beat furiously at his lap, sending the cup, the butt, and the ashes into the street.

~

Emma opened her eyes as she changed poses and caught a sudden movement below her window. She didn't recall ever seeing anyone in the alley and it took a moment to register the blue Corvette. She dropped to a crouch to avoid being seen, but kept her eyes on the car. Terrified and fascinated she watched the driver's door open, followed by a blur of frantic movements behind the windshield and a coffee cup skittering across the gravel.

"What the . . . ?" A second later, she dashed to the phone, dialed Finn's number, and waited. Ten rings. No answer. Emma returned the phone to the bedside table and frowned. She sneaked up to the window, carefully avoiding the incoming sunlight, and peeked out. The Corvette was gone. She returned to the bed, decided there was nothing else she could do, and prepared to dress for work. She took her watch from the table and fastened it on her left wrist over a small tattoo.

~

Finn opened the door into Philippe's office and braced himself for confrontation. A few moments ago he'd turned on his phone and saw the missed calls from Emma.

"It's almost 10:00. I've been trying to call you." Emma's voice trembled. "That blue car was watching me this morning. In my bedroom for Christ's sake!" She stood before him, arms by her side, her fists opening and closing. Finn glanced at Dan on the couch by the coffee table and turned back to Emma. He cleared his throat.

"I didn't think they'd be back so soon."

"What happened to, you're-supposed-to-watch-over-me?"

"Sorry. I should have stayed there last night." Would he ever get this right? He wondered whether he'd been away too long. Whether he'd lost interest in returning to his past life or in keeping a step ahead of the enemy, whoever they were.

"Finn, I'm scared. You've got to figure this out."

He nodded and gestured toward the coffee table. Emma sat on the couch beside her brother. Finn took the nearest chair.

"Just a thought," he said. "Roscoe was afraid of Philippe. Now that he's gone, Roscoe's on full point."

"You think it was Roscoe?" Emma curled her lips in disgust.

"Not sure," Finn answered.

"Can't you do something?" her eyes pleaded.

"There's only so much I can do if it is Roscoe."

Dan's jaw dropped.

"Philippe made me promise to lay off him." Finn rubbed the fingers of one hand across his forehead.

"Yeah?" Dan turned to his sister with a told-you-so expression. "Why are you here, anyway?"

"To tell you that Roscoe's bid for Xanthus is a front for Logan."

They both turned to him with their mouths open.

"No wonder Roscoe stalled," Dan mused.

"He probably had to get the okay," she glanced at Dan.

"Logan's a shareholder. It would make sense for him to want the rest of the business," Dan said.

"He's got a horse in this race," Emma added.

"Logan told me he didn't think Xanthus was particularly valuable," Finn said.

"Probably why he sent Roscoe to make an offer," Dan said. "Didn't want people to know he thought otherwise."

"Logan's giving Roscoe the money?" She sought confirmation.

"Logan's broke," Finn said.

"Then how's he planning to buy Xanthus?" Dan asked.

"Broke doesn't mean he can't borrow," Finn replied.

Emma eyed her brother. "Roscoe wants Xanthus, but has no money and he's unpredictable. Logan can lay his hands on millions and he is at least sane."

"I don't like Logan any better than I like Roscoe." Dan's lips curled.

"I know," Emma said. "Philippe had some use for the creep, but I never knew what it was. Still, if he wants Xanthus, this is our chance to get out of it in one piece."

"What have we got, though?" Dan held out empty hands. "An investment firm with no capital. Philippe stole it. Xanthus is worthless."

"Logan's no fool," Finn said.

Emma looked at Finn. "But he must have a powerful reason for wanting Xanthus. And if he's using Roscoe as a front, he doesn't want us to know how badly he wants it. Plus, he doesn't know our situation."

Finn nodded agreement.

"I was present last year when a group of analysts interviewed Philippe." Emma looked at both men. "I think I know how to bait the hook for Logan." She stood, walked to the desk, and turned on the computer. Then she paused and looked up at Dan. "I'm also calling Paul from BrighTel. He will be happy to help us close the loop when I offer him an incentive."

"I'm skeptical," Finn said.

"What do you mean?" Emma sat up straight in her chair.

"There's something going on we don't understand. Logan says the business isn't worth anything, but he sends Roscoe to buy it." He looked back and forth between brother and sister. "Why Roscoe?"

"Roscoe told me he's the only one who understands the business," Dan said. "Maybe Logan is just looking out for his own interest."

"I don't like it," Finn said. "Logan is a slippery customer." He turned to Emma. "Maybe Logan thinks once he gets Xanthus, he can find the missing money?"

"Technically, if he buys Xanthus and the stolen money turns up, it will belong to him," Dan said.

"If you believe the money will turn up, that, by itself, is a good reason not to sell Xanthus," Finn said.

"But what if it doesn't turn up? Emma asked. "Then we're sitting on nothing."

Finn sat back and regarded the siblings. "Whatever you believe, insofar as the missing money's concerned, is one thing. But I think something bigger is going on here and I'd recommend you don't sell Xanthus until we know what that is."

"I agree with Finn," Dan said.

Emma looked from one to the other. "We're going to sell. I have a plan."

"Okay," Finn said. *I'm wasting my time.*

~

Emma gave full attention to the computer and Finn decided to pay Roscoe another visit. He left the office, started down a corridor, and heard footsteps behind him.

"You keeping your eyes on the ball there, stud?" Dan asked. "Cause you don't seem to be keeping up."

Finn didn't bother to look. "When it comes to your sister, I've got the ball."

"I see. That's why she left you."

Finn was tiring of Dan's taunts. He slowed, took a step into Dan's space, and looked him in the eye.

"Look, we get along fine."

"So you're gonna stick with her this time?"

"She left because I couldn't give her what she wanted. My fault, but I'm dealing with it."

"Yeah, Myrna told me."

Finn looked away and shook his head at Dan's naiveté. Then he looked back into his eyes. "As long as Roscoe pays her rent, you'll get all the pink taco you can handle."

Dan backed away. A sneer came to his lips. "You are as vile as people say."

~

Allegra allowed Hedges to hold the door to the City View Restaurant. She led them into the bright, open dining room. She immediately encountered a young and very prim Chinese hostess who smiled and gestured to a table for two. Hedges held the chair facing the door while she lowered her body and slid her knees beneath the crisp white table cloth. He took the seat opposite and smiled at her.

A steady stream of dim sum carts rolled by their table and Allegra selected a few baskets and sampled them cautiously. The detective seemed pleased with her modest effort to explore the unfamiliar food even though she couldn't hide her distaste. She grew anxious about their leisurely pace during an important investigation and was about to say something when it dawned on her that he was making a special effort to be kind and expressing misgivings would be rude. She asked instead whether he had spoken with Logan.

"He was not happy to discuss Kassar," Hedges answered. "But he acknowledged being a minority shareholder in Xanthus. He suspects that Kassar was stealing from the company."

"Do you think is true?" She looked up from her food.

"One way or another, money is the root of this crime."

"So maybe it is Kassar who get money from Logan, as you say last night." She rolled a shrimp dumpling in a dish of soy, chili, and Chinese mustard, hoping to disguise the taste.

"Do you think Kassar's nationality has any bearing?" He set his chopsticks on his plate and waited.

She raised one eyebrow. "How it make difference?

"I don't know." Hedges shrugged. "I'm asking you."

Creases formed on her forehead while she chewed the dumpling. Finally, she swallowed and looked across the table at Hedges. "Lebanese are good businessmen. He make a lot of money?"

"Good, but not great."

"But if he steal money, then we look at Lebanese banks." She saw a question flicker to his face. "More secretive than Swiss," she explained. "No agreement with American tax authority."

"Um," Hedges nodded. "Like I said, it's about the money.

But murder is crime of passion, she told herself. *Why does he not see that?*

~

Logan glanced at the caller ID on his phone and rubbed the back of his neck. No way could he ignore the call.

"Hello, Mister Park."

"Roscoe says he does not have a deal yet for Xanthus. What are you doing?"

Logan took a deep breath. "We're negotiating. They want fifty mil."

"Don't worry about the price, Logan."

"I have to worry. I'm the one coming up with the money. If I have to borrow it, I'll have to pay it back."

"You will be able to pay it back. No problem."

Logan put a smile in his voice. "Mister Park, if you're so confident, why don't you buy Xanthus?"

"Sorry, Logan. I cannot be any part of it. That is why I came to you."

"I don't understand why the mystery."

"I can't be involved with Xanthus' business, that's all. The big customers won't permit it."

"Still not sure I understand."

"Xanthus ships things that are subject to export control restrictions. It can't have foreign ownership."

"I see."

"Good. Now please move quickly. Just remember how much money you are going to make. Remind Roscoe that he will have his business once again. The big customers will have uninterrupted service. Everyone will be happy."

"Mister Park, what happens if we can't make a deal with Emma Kassar?"

Holliday's voice took on a hard edge. "You will make a deal, Logan."

Logan didn't like the menacing tone or the direct order, but he knew when to shut up. "I'll talk to Roscoe."

~

Finn left Xanthus at 101 California and crossed Market Street. He took the escalator to the underground BART station where he boarded the Third Street light rail for Hunter's Point. He reached the Evans Avenue station at noon, disembarked, and walked the two blocks to R&P Tool and Die. The short walk in the open air felt good. He arrived at R&P and saw that the front entrance was locked. *Maybe they're at lunch.* Finn hoped to catch Roscoe by surprise and didn't want to ring the bell. He decided to look for a rear entrance and ducked around the end of a chain-link fence into the adjoining empty lot. Picking his way through tall weeds and discarded trash, he saw a large building standing on the far side of the lot to his right and, to his left, the steel Quonset of R&P Tool & Die connected at the rear to a two-story annex that extended to Fairfax Avenue at the back of the lot. He wondered whether Roscoe owned the adjacent property. If he had that much money, why did he want Xanthus? Why did Roscoe and Logan want Xanthus? What was the connection to Philippe's murder?

Finn walked to the far corner of the annex and turned left into a small parking lot. He saw there was another entrance to R&P from Fairfax Avenue. The blue Corvette was parked in the dirt between him and a door into the annex. Finn stopped and swore under his breath, "Roscoe, you son of a bitch."

He glanced around and saw no one. The 'vette had backed into a parking space below a row of windows and was the only vehicle present. Finn guessed Roscoe was probably at a desk somewhere inside if he wasn't at lunch. He would chance that no one was working in the annex. He stole up to the passenger door of the 'vette and and squatted down to look in the window. Even through tinted glass he could see a jumble of eight-by-ten photos lying on the passenger seat. They looked like surveillance photos but in color: A woman getting dressed, shot with a telephoto lens from outside her bedroom window. However, one picture was a full-face enlargement and Finn instantly recognized Emma. Suddenly, the promise to go easy on Roscoe fell away like a broken shackle.

"You fucking perv," he said to himself. Finn reached for the car-door handle. At the same time he heard the rear door of the annex burst open. He stood and looked over the car. Roscoe came thundering toward him, his face red with rage. Finn waited. Roscoe charged at full speed around the front of the car, but his momentum carried him wide.

Finn scooted around the trunk to the driver's side and looked over the top at Roscoe. "That was you who tried to run me over two nights ago. Cocksucker."

"If I'd known it was you, I'd of left faggot slime all over the road, you piss ant piece of shit." Roscoe gathered for another charge: clenched his teeth, pumped his arms, and accelerated around the trunk. Again he turned wide and missed Finn, who sidestepped around the hood to the passenger side.

Roscoe stopped by the driver's door. His face was red. He sputtered, "Fuck you, Hauk." Finn knew that as long as he kept him enraged, Roscoe couldn't catch him.

Roscoe also realized his error. He reversed direction, walked around the trunk, and then sped up to a fast but controlled pursuit. Finn also reversed direction and danced away from the big man, keeping the 'vette between them.

"I'm on to you, pervert," Finn shouted as he came again around the trunk to the passenger's side.

"Oh yeah? Then why are you running, faggot?"

"This isn't running," Finn retorted as he skipped around the hood to the driver's' side. "This is making you sweat before I kick your ass."

"Not a chance, dickhead."

Finn heard the annex door open behind him. In front of him, over the 'vette, Roscoe stopped beside the passenger door. Finn halted and turned to face the annex. One of the burly mechanics from his last visit now ran toward him, his blue apron flapping, and his right hand clutching a two-foot section of round steel bar above his head. Finn automatically computed the man's closing speed and waited, motionless.

The muscles tensed in the man's face as he concentrated on swinging the steel rod at the right instant while running at full speed. Six feet from Finn he swung his big right arm, intending to land a crushing blow to his quarry's skull. At the moment the steel bar started to descend, Finn launched his body into the oncoming opponent with full force. He held his left hand out in front, stiff and flat like the blade of a spear. He flew inside the arc of the metal bar, which passed behind him, and felt his fingertips smash into the assailant's larynx just as the big man's momentum drove them both into the passenger side of the 'vette. They collapsed to the ground with Finn trapped under the mechanic who lay face up, clutching at his throat, fighting to breathe. Finn pushed at the man's head to roll the body off. Roscoe came around the front of the 'vette with a murderous look. Finn couldn't escape.

"No shit," Roscoe looked down and grinned. The assailant's head and shoulders still pinned Finn on his back. He kept pushing, but before he could free himself, Roscoe sneered, "I'm going to squash you like a bug," and pulled his right knee up to his chest, preparing to stomp on Finn's head. Finn had moved the assailant's head enough to roll onto his right side. He kicked his left foot with all his might at the leg supporting Roscoe's weight. The blow landed hard on the inside of Roscoe's knee, the leg caved, and the former basketball player toppled to the ground beside Finn.

Finn rolled from under the assailant and scrambled to his feet. He glowered at Roscoe who lay on his side facing him, clutching his injured leg to his chest. With his right foot, Finn stomped on the ankle of Roscoe's other leg. The big man bellowed.

"That ought to keep you off your feet for a while you retarded freak." he shouted.

"Fuck you, Hauk," Roscoe spit the words between groans of pain.

Finn kicked him in the gut. "You tried to kill me!" Roscoe groaned. Finn kicked him again. "Moron!" Roscoe's face twisted in agony. Finn made himself take several deep breaths. His voice was calm when he spoke again. "Look, asshole. I know what you're trying to do to Emma."

"Faggot," Roscoe glared at him.

"I am here to make sure nothing happens to her." He paused to see whether Roscoe was listening. "So, Logan wants to buy her business, fine. But you. Uh-uh. She doesn't want to see your face or hear your voice again."

Roscoe lay in the dirt. Both hands cosseted the injured knee against his chest. He looked back at Finn, eyes burning with hate.

Finn kicked the knee. Roscoe howled in pain. Finn stomped again on the exposed ankle. Again Roscoe howled.

"Do you understand?" Finn said through his clenched teeth.

Roscoe groaned. He coughed. He did both at the same time.

"Look at me and say you understand," Finn repeated. He could see Roscoe trying to speak between coughs. The sound of an approaching car made Finn look up at the street. A black suburban stopped at the curb and two men in suits stepped out. Finn watched as they approached. They looked official.

"You Finn Hauken?" asked the nearest man when he had closed to dozen feet.

So much for low profile. Finn stared hard into the approaching face. "Who's asking?"

"Bureau of Industry and Security, " the agent replied. He held his ID out in front of him. "Are you Mister Hauken?"

"Yes, I am."

"You know a Daniel Emmonds?" the agent asked.

"I do." *That idiot told me he was sending these assholes.* "You want to talk about Xanthus, right?"

"Would you mind coming with us?" The agent pointed to Roscoe. "You can leave him. This shouldn't take long."

Finn nodded, brushed the dirt from his cloths, and stepped around Roscoe who hissed up at him from the dirt, "You're dead pussy, Hauken."

~

Roscoe watched Finn depart in the black SUV and let rage thunder through his body. It lessened the pain from his legs. After several tries, he managed to roll onto his right knee. Standing was impossible. He couldn't put his full weight on the right ankle. He looked at the machinist, who was sitting up and could breathe again. Roscoe beckoned him for help so he could limp back inside the annex. The machinist supported him with one hand, keeping the other on his own throat. He couldn't speak, but Roscoe cursed Finn with every step.

Once inside the office, Roscoe showered and changed. He iced the injured joints. As soon as he could walk, Roscoe got into the Corvette and headed downtown. He drove up the 280 on-ramp at Twenty-Fifth Street, took out his phone, and dialed Logan's number. The broker was not happy to hear about the latest confrontation with Finn and unloaded over the phone.

"The guy was being a pain."

Logan would have none of it. "How are we supposed to lock this down if you keep blowing your cool?"

"What was I supposed to do? He was looking in my car."

"Act like nothing happened. He can't hurt you."

"I had photos in there."

The phone remained quiet for a few moments. When Logan spoke again his voice had a chill, "What kind of photos?"

"Just the pretty wife," Roscoe tried to sound meek.

"What the hell, Roscoe?"

"It was nothing. I like the bitch and I was watching, so I snapped a few."

"Yeah. I can imagine."

Logan's contempt angered Roscoe, but he was unprepared for what came next.

"Roscoe, I think it's time you disappeared for a while."

"What do you mean?"

"Well, you were supposed to convince Emma to sell Xanthus, but your crude behavior has compromised our position."

"I can still get her to sell."

"Maybe. But you're getting Hauken all riled up and I don't want him screwing up the deal."

"Fuck Hauken"

"You can say that, but I sure as hell don't want him on my ass."

"Don't worry about Hauken. I'll talk to Emmonds. Get him to convince her. I can do it. You'll see." Roscoe waited for Logan's acknowledgement, but the broker stayed silent for a long time. Finally, he spoke.

"Roscoe, I think this is an excellent time for you to become a missing person."

"What?" He couldn't believe it. "What about Xanthus?"

"Things aren't working out as planned. I think I better take it from here."

"Do I still get to run it?" His voice grew squeaky. "Holliday said I was going to run it."

"It's getting complicated. I need to discuss it with Park."

"You can't just kiss me off, Logan. Holliday wants me part of this deal."

"We'll just have to let things work out, Roscoe. Maybe Park can find something else for you until we get everything settled."

Roscoe slammed his mobile down on the console. "Motherfucker!" He floored the accelerator. The 'vette dropped a gear and a second later accelerated past 100 mph. "Fuck it." Roscoe whizzed past the slower moving vehicles. "That cocksucker Emmonds better come around."

~

Logan lowered his mobile and set it on the counter next to a protein drink the health club's barista had just served him. He looked over at Myrna. Her face was flushed. Sweat soaked her spandex workout gear. He couldn't help eyeing the outline of her nipples. He suddenly wanted to take her home. Roll around while they were both hot and sweaty from working out. He almost forgot Roscoe.

"He's sick." She curled her upper lip.

The fantasy vanished. "I had to do it. He's a God damned loose cannon."

"Good. I'm glad. I hate the fuck."

"Only thing is," Logan ran a towel over his sweating brow. "I've got to figure another way to get Xanthus before Monday."

"What's the rush?" The barista delivered Myrna's protein drink.

"An analyst I know called me earlier. He says one of its investments is about to pay off big time. Something I knew about. But he says it's going to catch fire."

Myrna was about to sip her drink, but stopped and looked at Logan. "Funny, Dan was saying something about a client that had to do with mobile phones."

Logan slapped the bar. "BrighTel! I knew it."

"That's it?"

"Yeah," Logan looked away, thoughtful. "The Fed has an announcement on Monday." Then he looked back at Myrna and gave her a familiar squeeze and a perfidious smile. "I need to know if that's what they're working on."

"Why not call Emma and ask her? You're a stockholder."

"I'd rather she didn't know my intention, yet. It's all about negotiating position."

Myrna set her drink back on the counter and turned to him with a gorgeous smile. "Just for you, baby."

~

Dwight held the rear door and Logan sank into the plush leather inside the Lexus. It was good to relax after a workout and let someone else worry about traffic. But he needed to make use of his time. Logan removed the mobile from his pocket, hit speed dial, and waited for his accountant-slash-troubleshooter, Kishore Menon, to answer.

"Logan. What's up?"

"That BrighTel deal Xanthus has an option for 51 percent of their stock."

"Is that good?"

"BrighTel will get approval from the Fed on Monday to buy a large chunk of wireless spectrum."

"Ah. You believe their stock will go up."

"If I can get the rest of Xanthus, I can nail controlling interest in BrighTel and that spectrum."

"That sounds like a good opportunity."

"If we can do it, I don't want some competitor stealing it at the last minute. I need fifty mil."

"I don't know how you could do that, my friend."

"C'mon, Kishore. Think of something."

Logan waited through the ensuing silence. Finally, Menon said, "I'll have to call you back."

Logan set the mobile on the seat next to him and waited. In all likelihood, Roscoe had blown the deal with Emma and he'd have to find a way to revive it. Go, Myrna baby. Emma had never seemed particularly friendly to him. But she wouldn't turn down a straightforward deal that would put money in her pocket, especially if, as he suspected, she didn't know Kassar had hidden away a fortune. Kassar must have left a clue to its whereabouts even if it was only to remind himself if he forgot. An account number. A pass code. Something. Once he got his hands on the business, he could search the records as long and deep as it took. If it was there, he'd find it.

But even if that didn't happen, Xanthus held an option for BrighTel's stock at a fixed price. Of course, Emma knew that BrighTel's stock value would soar on Monday, once the Fed announced the spectrum award. But she lacked the cash to exercise Xanthus' fixed-price option in order take the profit when the stock price skyrocketed. *We'll make her an offer she can't refuse*, he laughed to himself. How many times does someone get to say that? His mobile sounded and Logan grabbed it on the first ring.

"Kishore. Listen, here's what I'm thinking. Xanthus is worth fifty mil today. After Monday's announcement, it will go up to maybe seventy or eighty. But guess what. Number one, they don't have the cash to exercise their option on BrighTel. Number two, Emma doesn't know squat about spectrum. She would let BrighTel use it for their own customers. But I know some industry guys who can unload that spectrum in a week for probably two hundred mil to the people who are desperate for broadband. Now, does that sound like a deal or what?"

"Why would she want to sell if she knows the company will be worth more tomorrow?"

"I'll offer her fifty mil today. She'll keep half and give half to BrighTel to secure their purchase. She'll go for the sure thing and I'll have control over the spectrum."

"But what if she decides to sell the spectrum herself?"

"I told you. She doesn't know diddily about BrighTel, let alone where to unload spectrum. I'm just going to simplify her life and make her rich."

"What makes you so sure Xanthus will purchase the BrighTel spectrum?"

"I'm investigating that as we speak."

"You have two properties that could get you thirty mil if you sign them over. What about the other twenty?"

"Talk to me, Kishore."

There was a long pause before Kishore spoke. "I can ask the pension fund. But it is with greatest reluctance, my friend. Perhaps they will be willing to add it to what you owe already and extend the deadline—"

"Kishore, you're worth every penny."

"But not long. Thirty days, maybe. Are you sure you can handle it?"

"With two hundred million? No problemo."

"You know what happens if you default? Even if, God forbid, you should go to prison, they will find you."

"I can do it," Logan shot back with confidence. "Set it up so the funds can move first thing Monday."

"You're sure? I don't want you getting in the river over your head."

Logan paused. Better safe than sorry. "Yeah. But give me a minute. My assistant's going to call me right back and then I'll confirm."

"I'll wait 'til I hear from you, Logan, but please remember, it's only a possibility."

~

Dan held open the conference room door for Myrna. He was hoping she would visit. They strolled to one end of the large table and stood together, holding each other's forearms. She kissed him with measured passion. He smiled brilliantly.

"I came by to ask you a question," she said. "My friend Sally offered me her reservation at The French Laundry for tonight. I know how much you like their food."

The smile melted on Dan's face. "That's wonderful Myrna. But I don't think I can get away."

Her lips grew pouty. "It takes ages to get into their dining room. I thought you'd be thrilled."

"I am. Indeed, I am. But tonight I've got important work to do."

Myrna reached a hand up to stroke his face. "Baby, I know how much you like The French Laundry. Whatever. It must be something big to keep you."

"The company's going all out, preparing for an announcement on Monday." Dan lowered his eyes. He knew she wanted to hear about it. Her hands dropped to his forearm.

"I hope it's good news for you," she said and squeezed with both hands.

"It has nothing to do with me."

She looked into his eyes with puzzlement.

Dan stepped back. Their arms fell to their sides.

"One of the clients." He slid his hands into his pants pockets. "The Fed is going to let them bid on more wireless spectrum."

Her eyebrows furrowed.

"Well, let's just say it's big." He stepped closer. "If they succeed, they'll control a significant share of the market. Their stock value will shoot up and Xanthus will be worth lots more money."

Myrna pulled him closer and kissed him playfully. "That much? Worth more than a night with me at The French Laundry?"

"If it goes through," he took her shoulders. "I'll get them to buy you a week of dinners at The French Laundry."

She pouted again. "Pooh. I'll just have to see if Sally will go in your place."

"Sorry."

Myrna stepped back, turned to leave, and smiled sweetly over her shoulder. "Bye."

Dan stood stiff and mute while she closed the door. Then he lifted his right hand, punched the air above his head, and let out a forced whisper. "C'mon, Logan."

~

Logan took one of the leather chairs in Philippe's office and prepared for battle, the kind of battle he was good at.

Emma sat behind Philippe's desk. It was mid-afternoon and she looked exhausted. *She must have sleepless nights mourning her husband*, Logan thought. Yet, she had called him and that increased his leverage. He looked into her swollen eyes with an exaggerated compassion.

"I'm astonished that you called me to do this today. It must be terribly difficult."

Emma nodded. "I wish you'd come direct."

He bowed his head. "You're right, of course. Please forgive me. I should never have involved Roscoe."

Emma's red eyes pleaded with him. "It's been too much. The stress . . . Philippe . . . I have to get away, Logan. Let someone else have the headaches."

He leaned forward. "You're sure?"

Her eyes filled with tears. "If you can meet my price."

Logan sat straight in the chair. "You said fifty mil."

Emma reached into a desk drawer and removed a box of Kleenex. She took one, blotted her eyes and looked at him. "Dan told me that BrighTel would receive a larger allocation of radio spectrum than the Fed had first proposed. It will double their value."

Logan leaned back and tried to mask the tension building inside him. But his eyes hardened. "Emma. You don't have the cash to give them. It doesn't make any difference to you how much spectrum they can buy."

She rested both hands on the desktop and smiled. "You're right. But you stand to make a lot more money than we originally forecast, a fortune, and I want a taste of that."

"What is a taste?"

"Make it seventy-five. I can payoff what Xanthus owes, BrighTel has enough to take full advantage of the Fed's generosity. You will make a bundle and I can walk away with no regrets."

Logan let his eyes grow large. "What does Xanthus owe? The last report I saw, you were flush."

Emma cupped her hands over her mouth. "Logan, I'm not going to sell you a pig in a poke. Philippe made a couple of bad calls in the last few months and he borrowed against future earnings from the BrighTel deal."

"How much?"

"About forty million."

"That means Xanthus is barely worth anything."

"It's also why the BrighTel deal is so important. It will make us whole. Then it will bring in more than we've ever made."

Logan's eyes defocused while he calculated in his head. He knew Philippe had stolen but the amount stunned him. He'd hoped it was substantial, but small enough to recover easily. Not forty million. Still, with BrighTel deal he stood to make a sizable profit even if he never found the missing funds. But it wasn't going to be easy. He refocused and saw Emma waiting, motionless, staring into his face. "You want me to give up prized real estate for this?"

"It's fair, Logan. You'll make a fortune and it's the right thing to do. Look at all that I've lost."

Logan sat, expressionless, for several moments. His voice conveyed no emotion when he spoke, "Fifty-five. A small concession to acknowledge your recent misfortune."

Emma stared back at him. Her eyes began to fill with tears again.

"I wouldn't do this for anyone else," he said softly.

After a few moments, Emma nodded, "All right." She placed her hands in her lap and straightened her back. "Ready when you are."

Logan opened his laptop. Emma swiveled in her chair to face the monitor on her desk. He began typing. "Okay. I send the order for transfer now. The bank won't deposit funds in BrighTel's account until 7:00 am Monday, start of business."

"Right. BrighTel informs us they have the money, we record the certificates—"

"I own Xanthus."

"And BrighTel has capital to buy spectrum the moment it goes public."

They nodded agreement. Logan closed his laptop. Emma switched off her computer.

"You're lucky to get in under the wire," she said.

"I'm obliged. And you?"

"Relief. Peace."

"For your sake, I hope so." Logan struggled to quell the uneasy thought of borrowing from the pension fund to meet her price.

~

Roscoe listened to the Doors because he liked the way Morrison's voice propelled him into a state of manic anticipation. Hated the whiny organ. He would crank up the volume except that loud music would attract passerby's attention to the blue Corvette, and its driver, parked on a quiet residential cul-de-sac. In the past half hour, he had watched a dozen Latino nannies wheel their charges past his car to Duboce Park, located behind him, at the end of the street. The fog had not rolled in yet and the temperature was still moderate. In the rear view mirror he could see Dan Emmonds driveway, four houses away. Through the windshield, he would spot his arrival when his car turned on to the cul-de-sac.

He didn't have to wait long. Emmonds' grey SUV could have been late for dinner by the way it sped into view and stopped abruptly on sidewalk in front of his home. Like the other houses on the street, Emmonds' garage was under the house, down a short, steep driveway. When residents were in a hurry, they frequently parked the front half of the car on the driveway and left the rear blocking the sidewalk. Like Emmonds did now. Roscoe watched him open the back of the SUV, grab an armful of grocery bags, and head up the front steps into the house. He had left the hatch open and would return for another load. Roscoe exited the Corvette and prepared to convince Emmonds that it was time to sell Xanthus.

~

At the same time Roscoe got out of his car, Finn crossed the open field in Duboce Park on his way to Dan's home. The Bureau of Industry and Security agents had escorted him from their office in San Jose after he convinced them he had no useful information. He needed to tell Emma that Roscoe was her mystery stalker and that hostilities had escalated because of his confrontation. He also needed to warn Dan.

Finn had stopped at a Taqueria across the street long enough to call Xanthus and learn that Emma had gone home. She'd probably stop for dinner, he thought. Roscoe wouldn't know where she was. He'll go to her home. Finn would be there, ready.

On his way to Emma's, he could warn Dan. He ordered a burrito to go, then walked to Diridon station and grabbed bus and rail connections to Duboce and Noe, guessing that he would arrive at Dan's at about the time he got home for dinner.

He stepped from the park onto the cul-de-sac. A commotion on the sidewalk ahead caught his attention, but he couldn't see it through the greenery, parked cars, sixty-gallon plastic trash bins, and assorted toys that cluttered his path. He walked faster and after a dozen steps recognized Roscoe's voice. Now, he saw the open tailgate of Dan's grey SUV hanging out over the sidewalk in front of his house. *Uh-ho, this can't be good.* Finn started to jog and swung out into the middle of the street for a better view.

Roscoe loomed head and shoulders over Dan. Groceries and torn brown paper bags littered the sidewalk. He couldn't hear their words, but there was no doubt of Roscoe's aggression as he came forward or Dan's fear as he backed away. The next thing Finn saw was a lazy roundhouse from Roscoe topple Dan to the pavement. Finn broke into a sprint. He cut between two parked cars, but tripped over a plastic refuse can he didn't see. It spun down the sidewalk. He staggered for several steps, but recovered his balance. Roscoe leaned over Dan. He looked up at the clatter and instantly recognized Finn. "Stay out of it, asshole!"

Finn closed rapidly, but Roscoe ignored him. He looked down at Dan who rolled slowly on the ground beside his car. Roscoe delivered three quick, vicious kicks to Dan's face. Before he could send another, Finn launched himself in a cross body block, hoping to knock Roscoe off his feet. This time, Roscoe was prepared. He braced himself. As Finn was about to slam into him, he grabbed Finn's body and spun sideways, allowing the body's momentum to carry it around him and onto the front steps of the house behind. "You're pissing me off, faggot," he barked as Finn got to his feet after a bruising landing on the steps.

Roscoe didn't wait for Finn's next move, but walked briskly to the Corvette. Finn took two steps after Roscoe and stopped. He glanced to his side at Dan writhing on the pavement. Dan's face was unrecognizable. His head lay in a pool of blood. Finn ran over and squatted beside him. Dan tilted his head slightly and tried to look at him, but his eyes weren't tracking together.

"You chased him off," his voice was raspy. He could barely speak. He let his head fall back into the blood.

"Not hardly."

"He left," Dan mumbled. He didn't move his jaw.

"Sorry I wasn't faster."

Dan brought one arm slowly up and touched his face. "Jesus, this hurts."

Finn bent closer. "Let me look."

Dan rolled only a few degrees. Finn saw crushed, bloody features, the mangled nose, the wide gash from his jaw to his crown. Grayish brain tissue glistening in the wound. "You look like shit."

Dan's lips parted. Finn couldn't tell whether it was an attempted smile or a grimace of pain. His voice sounded dry, "What're you doing here, anyway?"

"Came to warn you about Roscoe." He placed a hand on Dan's shoulder. "I'm just sorry I was too late."

"Didn't think he'd get violent."

Finn glanced at the Corvette and then back at Dan. "He won't again, if I have any say."

He saw Dan trying to move.

"Stay calm."

Finn heard the Corvette peal out.

"He wants Emma." It was a hoarse whisper. Then Dan's eyes stopped moving. Finn heard the squeal of the Corvette rounding the corner.

"Fuck. Fuck!" He punched the sidewalk with both fists. He threw his head back and screamed at the grey SUV. **"Fuck!"** Then he looked again at Dan. Lifeless. No doubt. Finn hung his head. His hand squeezed the shoulder unconsciously. He remained still with his eyes closed while he breathed, while his mind tore after the Corvette.

Another minute, then he pulled Dan by his hands up to a sitting position, stooped down under one arm, and lifted him gently into a fireman's carry and hauled him to the door open on the porch. "Christ," he said out loud. He thought of Emma unknowing and in danger. Of not leaving Dan on the sidewalk. Of Roscoe's head start. *You won't get away, you son of a bitch.*

~

Allegra followed Hedges through the red and blue flashing lights of the squad cars, under the yellow and black crime scene tape, past the uniformed policemen on guard duty, up the porch steps into Dan Emmonds' home. Inside, more blue-clad officers searched the rooms and furnishings. Two Paramedics waited beside a gurney in the living room. Dan's corpse lay on its back, its dull eyes staring up at the ceiling from the crushed face covered in dried blood. The detective and the attorney moved to opposite sides of the gurney and leaned over it to examine the corpse.

Allegra turned her body so Dan's face was upright in her vision and touched his shoulder tenderly. "Missus Kassar will be very sad."

Hedges nodded, adding, "The man who reported this said he saw Finn Hauken in the driveway."

Allegra looked at him. "Who is Finn Hauken?"

"A very violent young man, by all accounts." Hedges returned her look. "Worked for Kassar until a couple of years ago when he was accused of killing Kassar's partner, Younger Park. Detective Costello took him into custody but he escaped."

She nodded to indicate she understood and looked again at Dan with heartfelt sorrow. "Poor woman. First husband, now brother."

"Yes. This doesn't look good," Hedges said. "Two Xanthus men dead in the last two days." Allegra watched Hedges shake his head.

~

Finn struggled to control his desperation as he hurried along Evans Avenue toward R&P Tool & Die. He couldn't afford another mistake. Dan had died because of him. Because of his fight with Roscoe. Because he had taken too much time getting to Dan's home. He berated himself again for stopping at the Giro shop instead of hurrying to the Muni. Frustration made him manic. *Where is Roscoe?* Finn stormed to the front entrance of R&P. The door was locked.

He cut through the vacant side lot and saw light coming through a row of windows on the side of the annex. The lower panes were frosted but the upper ones were clear. A drain pipe ran beside the window. Finn shimmied up to the window and stood on the ledge. Through the clear glass, he saw the large shop with its security lights blazing. All of the machinery, lathes, drill presses, metal benders, routers, hydraulic presses, everything stood cleaned and idle. A windowed door lead into the Quonset. It was dark. The entire place looked deserted.

Finn jumped from the ledge and ran to the annex door. It was locked. He jogged back to the Muni station on Third Street. Each footfall pounded another shard of desperation into his heart.

~

Hedges listened to the voice of Detective Costello give him the best news he'd heard all day. With his right hand, he turned the unmarked cruiser onto Castenada and searched the street numbers painted on the curb for the address of the Kassar house. His left hand held the phone to his ear. He looked over at Allegra, but she was talking in Italian on her phone.

Hedges concentrated on Costello's voice while the car edged up the street. Occasionally, he issued an excited, "No shit." Allegra finished her call and tried to interrupt him. He waved her off so he could hear his conversation and continue to watch through the windshield for the street number of Emma's house. He finally terminated the call and glanced at Allegra. "Detective Costello," he said. She was on the verge of opening her mouth, but stopped. "Last night, he saw Kassar's ex-girlfriend, Myrna Hensik, with Finn Hauken, the guy who was reported at Dan Emmonds home when he was killed." He looked at her for reaction.

"He is suspect, then?"

"Certainly for Dan Emmonds."

"And Mister Kassar?"

"A fugitive wanted for murder? Seen with the victim's ex-girlfriend?"

"But your colleague did not arrest him?"

"By the time Costello confirmed the warrant, Hauken was gone."

Out of the corner of his eye, he saw her fidgeting with her phone. "Okay, what gives?" he asked.

"Is Romero. He say Mister Kassar die from stab wounds. In room where he is killed, they find bloody shoe marks. First, two men walk. Then, one man come later."

Hedges pulled to the curb in front of Emma's home, and thought for a moment. "That's a lot of traffic."

"Yes. But we should not tell to Missus Kassar."

He opened the driver's door, stood and looked back at Allegra. "I suppose. She's got enough now with her brother."

~

The maitre d' of the Emerald Rose stood at the head of the dining room. The 8:00 pm seating was sold out. His critical eyes searched both the customers for unspoken desires and the wait-staff for lapses in service. The restaurant's reputation depended on his skill, for which he was justifiably proud, the room having attained elite status within San Francisco's Financial District. His reverie was suddenly interrupted by the sound of the front door bursting opening behind him. Startled, the maitre d' turned and saw a disheveled man barge toward him with blood on his clothes and menace in his eyes.

The maitre d' had seen harried men before, many times. The jilted lover, the sore loser, the frustrated businessman. He glided to intercept the intruder swiftly, before he created a disturbance among the peaceful guests. The man stopped when the maître d' blocked his path. "May I help you sir?" His voice was barely polite. His face and body posture had the look of impenetrable stone.

Finn craned his head to a look past the maitre d' at the diners. "Roscoe Pender?"

"Yes, he dined with us," the maitre d' held firm. "But he left half an hour ago."

Finn didn't move, but completed his scan. "Say where he was going?"

"No sir."

Finn turned for the front door. The maitre d' relaxed and returned to his room, just another crisis to be attended and forgotten.

~

Finn waited on the stoop outside Emma's side door and prayed she was all right. The door cracked open as far as the chain lock would allow. She looked out. He knew he looked a mess. She made no move to open the door.

"What do you want?"

"I have some bad news, Emma. May I come in?" He saw her red and puffy face. Feared she already knew.

"The police just left. They told me about Dan."

"Emma," he screwed up his face. "I'm so sorry. I tried to get to him in time."

"The police . . . someone reported that you hit him and—" Her eyes beseeched him for the truth.

Roscoe, that son of a bitch. His body shook. Emma continued to implore him with her eyes.

"It was Roscoe. Outside Dan's house. He hurt him before I could stop it. Last thing Dan said, he was coming after you." Finn realized he was pleading. He looked away from her. His face grew taught and he turned in a slow circle. For the first time he could remember he wanted to kill someone. He looked into Emma's face again and wanted more than anything for her to understand. "I tried to warn him . . . I mean, I came as soon as I . . . you're all right?"

Emma slammed the door. Finn heard the chain lock. The door opened wide and she thrust herself into the space. "I'm fine. See?"

The bitter tone startled him. He stepped back.

"Now go." Her voice was loud. "Leave me alone. I'm sick of this."

Finn's jaw dropped. "Emma!"

"No." She stomped her foot. "Everything's going wrong, Finn. Dan wasn't supposed to die. You were supposed to help me, help us. If you'd taken care of Roscoe, Dan would still be alive."

Finn's grew stupefied and his face fell even further. "Emma." He reached out to take her arm, but she slapped his hand away.

"My brother is dead, Finn! I want to be alone. Do you understand?" She stepped back inside and slammed the door, harder this time. Finn was dumbfounded. He just stared into the dark wood. Words swirled in his head. *If I'd taken care of Roscoe? Of all people, she should know better.* He'd never felt so misunderstood. After several deep breaths, he retreated from the stoop and headed uphill to catch the Muni.

~

Roscoe sat in the blue Corvette downhill from Emma's door. He'd parked in a row of cars and knew Finn wouldn't see him even if he had looked back over his shoulder. Roscoe watched Finn trudge away and smiled to himself. *Fuck you, Hauk.*

SUNDAY

On Sunday, Allegra woke at noon. Hedges had told her to get some rest and recover from her jet lag, but the extra sleep hadn't helped. Waiting for him to collect her from the hotel lobby, she had felt more tired than at any time since her arrival. They didn't speak after driving away from the hotel, for which she was thankful, but she couldn't keep her eyes open waiting for Hedges to return from the convenience store. A tap on the passenger window woke her. Hedges stood beside the car with two sixteen-ounce coffee containers. She opened the window, smiled, and accepted the drink. Hedges walked around the car and took the driver's seat.

It wasn't espresso, but the hot liquid revived her quickly. Hedges, meanwhile, had set his cup on the dash and was leafing through a file. He glanced over at her.

"Guess who arrived at the San Francisco Airport the day after Kassar died?"

She took a sip of her coffee. "I did."

"Besides you."

She thought briefly about the graceful man who'd cavorted before them to get her attention. "I cannot guess."

Hedges leaned closer and held the file flat so she could see. She looked down at the photo. Her heart skipped. She jabbed her finger. "Is him?"

"That's Finn Hauken." The detective looked smug. "I knew the guy was trouble."

"At police station?"

"When I saw him at the airport."

Allegra frowned. She sipped her coffee. She didn't want to be disappointed, but couldn't help it. She lifted her head from the cup and looked out the passenger window.

Hedges seemed to understand. "Sorry."

"Maybe Hauken use fake passport to go to Italy."

"No. He didn't come through Customs and Immigration. But that doesn't mean he couldn't be our guy."

"How we will find him?"

"I'm thinking Myrna Hensik, Kassar's former girlfriend. Finn was with her Friday night." Hedges closed the folder and set it between them on the seat. She caught his sidelong glance as he turned the ignition key. "You won't believe her."

~

The more Nico pondered their mission, the more he believed they could kill the woman and escape the police. Alfonse had slept during the Alitalia flight from Rome while he had contrived a plan. They landed early and breezed through Immigration and Customs. Both held valid passports and carried only hand luggage. They took the tram to the car rental building on the north side of San Francisco International. Nico chose a red Ford Mustang and drove north on highway 101. The Mustang's GPS guided them around the city, along the Embarcadero to Fisherman's Wharf, to Mason Street, and finally to the Hotel San Remo. Nico's brother knew the owner.

He hunched over at a tiny table in the hotel's small, crowded bar and shared a bottle of Pinot Grigio with his friend. Nico pointed at the map spread on the surface between them and spoke to Alfonse in Italian.

"The company is here." He placed a dark stubby finger on the 101 California building. "My cousin says there will be a big announcement tomorrow morning. Everyone will arrive by 8:00." His finger moved to the entrance on Pine Street. "This is where we will wait."

"Where is the car?" asked Alfonso.

"Ah." Nico smiled. "Parking is under the building. There is a stairway from the lobby and we park the car by the door in the garage." Nico paused for a moment and then pointed to an icon for a BART station on Market Street across the intersection from 101 California. "But look. Here is the metro." His voice jumped an octave. "It will take us to the international terminal at the airport in twenty minutes. We finish our work. We disappear underground. We leave the car. Better, no?"

Alfonso continued to study the map for a long time. Eventually, he looked at Nico. "There are so many entrances to the building. How do we know which one to watch?"

Nico pointed again to 101 California. "The main one comes from the plaza in front." He moved his hand to Pine Street on the opposite side. "This one is less crowded, closer to the elevators in the lobby. I think we should be here."

Alfonso looked at his partner. "Probably, you are correct. But we must be prepared if she arrives by a different route."

~

Allegra followed Hedges down the narrow concrete steps to the sub-street-level entrance of a coral stucco building. She stood beside him while he lifted the heavy brass knocker and tapped three times. The dark wooden door opened a crack and Allegra saw a partial face, an attractive woman with red eyes and dark streaks of makeup on her cheeks. She seemed to recognize Hedges and opened the door, revealing a trim, richly-dressed figure. The woman clutched a rose colored handkerchief in one hand, parked the knuckles of her other hand on one hip, and glared at them with stone-cold eyes.

"You lose something?" She glared at Hedges.

"A friend saw you with Finn Hauken, evening before last," Hedges replied.

Myrna's eyes held fast. "Oh yeah, the poondangler."

"Couldn't hook up, eh?"

"Fuck you. I'm busy," Allegra couldn't believe the woman's cobalt eyes could get any colder. "What do you want?"

"Where's Hauken?"

"Who cares?"

"I care." The detective's voice changed to ice. "He's a suspect in a murder investigation."

"How should I know?"

"You knew Dan Emmonds, didn't you?"

Myrna stiffened. Allegra wondered why Hedges antagonized the woman.

"We think Hauken might have been involved in Philippe Kassar's death also. You wouldn't know anything about that, would you?"

Myrna didn't move a muscle.

Hedges took a step closer. "Where do you think he is?"

"Out searching for little boys?"

"Jesus," Hedges chuckled quietly. "I asked you a question!" He lifted his hand in a way that could have been threatening, but Myrna didn't budge. Allegra squeezed between them.

"Talk about Mister Kassar," she said.

Myrna scowled at Allegra and stepped back into her apartment. "He was old news before. He's rotten news now." She eased the door closed. "I gotta go."

No one in Italy could get away with treating the police like this, Allegra thought. She turned to Hedges.

"She knows we don't have a warrant." His jaw was tight.

They turned together and ascended the steps.

"What is poondangler?" Allegra asked.

"A guy who lets a girl think they're going to have sex and then doesn't go for it."

Allegra wondered whether Finn was really like that.

~

Anyone watching Finn stumble down Market Street in the early evening would have thought he was drunk. The glazed, unfocused eyes. He bumped pedestrians without noticing, stood motionless for minutes at a time or meandered a serpentine path along the sidewalk. A shop window caught his attention. The display of dried sticks, rocks, and sand made him think of snakes. He peered through the glass, but saw nothing, only a face reflected. Was this the picture Emma saw? Haggard? Without purpose?

His phone rang four times. Without taking his eyes from the window, he took it from his pocket, held it to his ear and waited. After a period of silence a woman's voice inquired, "Finn?"

"Yeah."

Her voice screamed from the earpiece, "That fucking Roscoe!"

Finn jerked his arm to get the noise out of his ear, waited a moment, then slowly returned the phone to his ear. The shout got his attention.

"You heard."

"That bastard!" He straightened his arm again, just as Myrna screamed. "That bleeding asshole!"

"Yeah."

"He called just to tell me what he did."

"It wasn't pretty." Finn looked down at the pavement. "How'd you get this number?"

He heard a long sigh. "Dan." Then short sobs. "I liked Dan. Why did Roscoe have to ruin it?"

"Well, you said it yourself: He's an evil prick."

Her voice was harsh. "I want you to fix his ass, God damn it. Isn't that what you do?

"Myrna—"

"Stop, Finn." She cut him off. "He's after you. He has Emma and he wants you.

Finn was suddenly alert.

"Emma?"

"He was blabbering like a maniac." She imitated Roscoe's voice, "Fucking Logan thinks he can have Xanthus without me? I'll show that ratfucker. Won't be anything left."

"Where is he?"

"How the fuck should I know. Ask Logan."

"On my way."

"The cops just left here," she cautioned. "They want you, too."

"Perfect."

~

Finn had to remind himself not to hurt Logan when he saw him across the weight room. He lay face up on a bench, straining beneath a one-hundred-eighty-pound barbell. Maybe he'd drop it on his neck. But not before Finn found out where Roscoe was. Logan lowered the barbell into the bench cradle above his head, grabbed the ends of the towel around his neck, and wiped the sweat from his eyes. He sat upright and looked in the mirrored wall. Finn saw Logan's face fall when he recognized him.

"Hauken. I thought we were done. What are you doing here?"

"Roscoe."

"What about him."

"You got a connection with him you didn't tell me about."

Logan's face grew pale. "Listen, Hauken. I had nothing to do with Roscoe's trip to Italy. He did that on his own."

A flash went off in Finn's mind. He hadn't guessed that Logan and Roscoe might be smart enough or bold enough to kill Philippe while he was out of the country. They must really want Xanthus. "I can't deal with that now, Logan. I've got to get to Roscoe. Where is he?"

Logan swiped a hand across his sweaty brow. He lowered his voice. "Roscoe's not your biggest problem, Hauken."

"What do you mean?"

"Remember Younger Park?"

"How could I forget? Half the world thinks I killed him."

"Don't worry about half the world. Just worry about Younger's brother, Holliday. He's in town and he wants revenge."

.Yeah. The Korean in the white Sprinter. He regarded Logan. "I'll worry about him later, too. Where's Roscoe?"

"How should I know?"

"He's got Emma."

Logan's brow furled. "I saw her yesterday at lunchtime. We made a deal for Xanthus."

"Congratulations. Apparently, Roscoe didn't get the word."

Logan shook his head. "No. He's out of it. I told him to disappear."

"He didn't take your suggestion."

Logan stood and began to pace around the weight bench. "Roscoe is an idiot. Totally unpredictable." His face screwed up as if a horrible picture formed his mind. "Jesus. Emma."

Finn glared at Logan. The veins throbbed on his forehead. Logan studied him. Evaluating? Fearful? He couldn't tell.

"I've got to find her," Finn's jaw tightened. He swayed on his feet

"You check his shop?" Logan asked.

"Last night. It was deserted."

"How about today? He doesn't have anywhere else to go."

Finn stopped moving. "Fuck! The shop."

~

Finn jumped from the light rail car when it stopped at 3rd and Evans and ran as soon as his feet touched the ground. There were few pedestrians in this neighborhood at nightfall. A good thing. A white man flying down the sidewalk in an all out sprint would be hard to ignore. Finn reached the R&P building in just over a minute and stood outside, out of breath, his mind racing, looking for a way inside. The entrance to the Quonset was locked tight. Steel grates protected the windows.

He scooted around the building into the vacant lot on the right and found an unbarred window. When the largest rock he could find didn't break the glass after two throws, he decided to try the annex door. He came around the corner of the building and saw no cars, no one around. The coast was clear. All he needed was a tool. Finn ran back around the corner and started searching the empty lot for something to help him open the annex door.

~

Murder has a logic to it, Hedges knew. Yet he was struggling to unravel the reasons behind Philippe Kassar's death. He sat in the cruiser with Allegra in front of the Starbucks on Ninth and Howard, a few blocks from the Hall of Justice. The only Starbucks in the area with off-street parking. Besides, Allegra had developed a taste for their mocha. He read to her from a folder open on his lap.

"Detective Costello arrested Hauken two years ago for murdering Younger Park. He made the collar, handcuffed him, and locked him in the back seat of his cruiser. Costello stepped away from his vehicle to talk with a patrolmen and when he returned. Hauken was gone."

"How he escape?"

"Detective Costello couldn't say," Hedges read the file. "He returned to the car and found it empty. The doors were all locked."

Allegra looked at Hedges and nodded. "You think he kill Mister Kassar?"

"He and Kassar were thick. He knew Kassar's business. We think he murdered his partner, Younger Park. He arrived at the San Francisco airport the day after Kassar died. He had enough time to kill him in Italy and return home via a different route. He's connected to all of the other people in this case."

She sensed his unspoken conclusion. "If he is not guilty, how he fit into crime?"

"Let's think about that. Kassar owned Xanthus. He bought it from Roscoe, who thinks he was swindled. Roscoe didn't kill Kassar out of revenge. Kassar's partner, Logan Evans, alibied him. So Roscoe and Logan are connected."

"Perhaps Logan Evans lie and Roscoe Pender go to Italy and kill Mister Kassar."

"Okay, so both men want Xanthus. Maybe why Dan Emmonds was killed also."

"But man who report Mister Emmonds' death say he saw Finn Hauken."

"Maybe they killed Dan Emmonds and blamed Hauken. In that case, maybe Hauken also didn't kill Younger Park. Let's say it was Logan or Roscoe or both who did."

"Logan and Roscoe want Xanthus and Hauken does not want them to have it."

"When I interviewed Emma, she said Xanthus was not tremendously valuable."

"Yes, but we see how much Logan and Roscoe want Xanthus," Allegra said.

"Why would Hauken want to prevent them from taking it? Unless Emma lied and Xanthus is worth a lot of money."

"We can ask Hauken."

Hedges shook his head. He threw the folder into the back seat and reached for the key to start the cruiser.

"Where do we go now?"

"We don't know where Hauken is. We do know where to find Roscoe. We'll check his business. If he's not there we'll check his home. I have a feeling those two will be in the same place soon."

~

Finn was frantic to find Emma before Roscoe could hurt her. He struggled to calm his mind while he scrounged the vacant lot looking for something to help him break into the annex. But he couldn't quell his fears. He was so consumed with purpose, he didn't notice the sage green Subaru Forester creep along Fairfax Avenue, pass the annex and drive away.

Finn also failed to notice Hedges park the cruiser on Evan Avenue in front of the R&P Tool & Die sign. Nor did he hear him bang on the door several times, then return to the car and drive away after receiving no response.

The only thought in Finn's mind was finding a way into the annex.

~

Logan couldn't recall feeling as fulfilled as he did this evening. He'd done everything he could to secure his future. Now, he just had to let the chips fall into place. He leaned back in the white leather couch and watched the gas flames curl around the clever arrangement of ceramic logs in his fireplace. The designers of his multi-million dollar condominium on Lombard Street had centered the fireplace on the west-facing wall between two floor-to-ceiling windows, each with its own stunning view: to the right, Alcatraz Island; to the left, the Golden Gate Bridge. The sun was low to the west and the play of lights around the Bay and the tranquility of the fire soothed his hyper-active mind. He sipped Louis Roederer Cristal Brut from a cut crystal champagne flute and turned to Myrna on the couch beside him. Her face looked swollen. Her fingers never stopped fidgeting.

"Not to worry, my dear. Everything's under control," he put his arm around her shoulders and drew her close.

Myrna leaned into him, but kept staring into the fire. "Except for Dan."

"That was cruel," he agreed.

"That fucker!"

"I think Hauken will solve that problem for everyone."

"Good fucking riddance."

"Then Holliday will solve the problem of Hauken."

She raised an eyebrow in his direction, "Oh yeah?"

Logan snorted. "Kassar told me that when he met Holliday, the man was spending eight hours a day in a Korean dojo. Guess he got mugged once and wasn't going to let it happen again. Anyway. At the moment, Hauken is totally focused on finding Emma. He'll never see Holliday coming."

"What if the cops get Hauken first?"

"They might. But we're good either way. Xanthus is in the bag and tomorrow all your dreams will come true." *And so will mine, you luscious bitch*. He squeezed her closer.

~

Finn found a piece of rebar. He hurried back around the corner of the building, almost to the entrance. He saw headlights approaching along Fairfax. He scooted behind a stack of wooden pallets near the curb and squatted down. The blue Corvette pulled up to the annex and stopped. Roscoe got out of the car, walked to the door, and inserted a key. Before he could push the door all the way open, Finn straightened up, took five swift, silent steps and slammed both hands into Roscoe's back, shoving him through the door and face first onto the shop floor.

Finn fell forward onto Roscoe's back, grabbed his hair, pulled back his head, and smashed it hard into the concrete. He felt the body go limp. He rocked back to his feet and stood over Roscoe, clenched his fists. He waited a few breaths to let his heart rate slow, then turned and shut the annex door.

In a row of bins along the wall adjacent to the door, he found a roll of electrical wire and ripped off a two-foot length. Roscoe was still out and he had no difficulty tying the man's hands behind his back. Finn grabbed Roscoe's feet and dragged him on his stomach across the concrete. The skin on Roscoe's forehead had split open. A smear of blood followed the body across the grey painted floor all the way to a sink on the back wall.

Finn turned on the faucet, rolled Roscoe over with his foot and splashed water into his face. Roscoe's eyes blinked. Finn knelt next to him, "Where's Emma?"

Roscoe needed several breaths before he could recall where he was. "Hauk. Glad you could make it."

"Where's Emma?"

Roscoe furrowed his brow as pain came over him. "You can't help her."

"I can. I will."

"Like you did with Dan?" he coughed, trying to laugh.

Finn punched hard. Again. A third time. He stood back, rubbed the knuckles of his right hand. Roscoe's eyes rolled in his head. They were glazed. Finn leaned down to check his condition. Roscoe turned his head toward him and spit in his face. Finn straightened and wiped away the spittle.

"Never mind. I'll find her myself." He stepped away and surveyed the shop. Down the wall from the sink where he stood was the door with a darkened glass panel he'd seen from the window ledge. It led to the offices in the Quonset. Finn hurried to the door and tried the knob. It was locked. He smashed the glass with his elbow, reached his hand through the break and pulled open the door.

~

Emma could not move. She could only shiver. Her hands and feet were bound to a hard chair in a pitch black room. Her slacks were soaked with urine. She was cold. She was afraid. The left side of her head ached where she'd been hit. Her tongue felt dried blood around her mouth.

The lecher had stolen into her home and grabbed her from behind while she was in the bedroom. She remembered hitting and biting her attacker and then nothing. She didn't know how long she'd been alone in the dark. Enough to pee her pants several times and rub her wrists and ankles raw on the bindings. Enough for her rage to solidify into icy fear. She couldn't stop the shaking of her body. He would return and then what? Rape her? Torture her? Kill her? What does that sick bastard want? Tears filled her eyes, the futility of being captured, made prisoner, by a man she absolutely detested.

She jumped at a sound. Pieces of glass falling on concrete. The only noise she'd heard since she'd found herself alone in the dark. Warm urine spread again through her seat. Her shaking grew so violent she thought the chair might tip over. She struggled to hear, but the blood rushed in her ears, overwhelming every other sound. Her teeth chattered. The chair vibrating beneath her. She wanted to cry for help.

Air moved over her face. Someone in the room. Close. She sobbed. She couldn't help it.

"Emma," came a whisper. Then someone stumbled into the chair and toppled them backward onto the floor. The person landed on her, but not with full weight. He had caught himself on his hands. She wasn't hurt. He moved off her and his hands touched her head, then her face.

"Emma?" she recognized Finn's voice and tried to speak. Her voice sounded muffled. His hands found the gag and pulled it away from her mouth.

"Finn," she sobbed. "Oh Finn." She was overcome with relief. It wasn't Roscoe.

"It's okay," he said. "Let me help you." His hands found hers and began to untie the rope that held them. She heard a loud clanging noise from another room. Finn stopped moving.

"Just a minute," he said. She felt him pull away. She was alone again in the dark.

~

Roscoe waited beside the open door for Hauken to come out. He held a length of metal bar in one hand. Blood from his cut forehead ran down the front of his body. When Hauken finally came through the door, Roscoe swung the bar. It hit Hauken in the chest. He fell backward and lay motionless, face up on the concrete. Roscoe went to the sink and grabbed a wet towel. He carried it to Hauken and wrung water onto the upturned face. He leaned over and leered as Hauken twisted his head to avoid the water. "Time to cut the bullshit, faggot."

Hauken looked back at him, "Or what? You gonna kill me like you did Philippe?"

The corners of Roscoe's mouth curled down. "He was already dead when I found him, the fat fuck."

Hauken began to squirm. That Roscoe didn't kill Philippe became clear to Finn just as Roscoe grabbed his ankles and dragged him across the floor. He thrashed, but Roscoe had him in an iron grip. He kept flailing his legs. Roscoe ran out of patience and kicked him viscously in the hip. Hauken yelled, but stopped squirming.

Roscoe grabbed a length of wire from the floor and lashed Hauken's ankles together. He flipped the victim onto his stomach, wrestled his arms behind his back, and wound more of the wire around his wrists. Beside the sink was a galvanized roller bucket with a mop standing upright in the water. Roscoe grabbed the handle of a mop and pushed the bucket next to Hauken. He rolled Hauken on his back, planted a foot in his stomach, reached into the bucket, withdrew a dirty wet rag, and threw it over Hauken's face.

Roscoe lifted the bucket and poured a steadily stream of dirty water over the rag. Hauken coughed. He made gagging noises. Roscoe watched him squirm, but the heavy foot he'd planted on Hauken's chest kept him from escaping. He started to cough uncontrollably. Roscoe kept pouring water on the rag. Hauken twisted his head back and forth to avoid the stream, but it did no good. The gagging sounds grew worse. He couldn't stop coughing. Finally the stream of water stopped. The bucket was empty.

Roscoe looked around and saw the enormous steel hook used by mechanics to lift heavy work and position it for the huge machines lined up in two rows down the center of the annex. The hook hung by a steel cable from a winch that could roll the length of the shop along a massive steel I-beam overhead. An operator controlled the hoist from an oblong box, suspended from a second cable near the hook.

Roscoe grabbed the control box and pulled the rig above Hauken. He pushed a button and lowered the hook to the floor. He looped the wire that bound Hauken's ankles over the hook then held down a button on the control box, raising Hauken upside-down until his head hung several feet from the floor. Hauken continued coughing and turned red. Roscoe heard him fighting to speak, "Roscoe! Fuck!"

Roscoe ignored him. He strode over to an acetylene welding rig and wheeled it back near Hauken. He grabbed the torch and igniter, unstrung the gas hoses from around the upright cylinders and approached Hauken from behind. Although Hauken struggled to twist himself around toward Roscoe, the thick cables from the winch prevented him from turning. Roscoe grabbed Hauken's shirt tail and pulled the garment down over his head exposing his naked back.

He gloated in anticipation.

~

Emma pushed the door with the broken glass aside and staggered into the shop. She saw Roscoe from the back, on his feet, looking down at his hands. Beyond him, to her horror, Finn hung upside down by his ankles. His hands were tied behind his back and he was twisting frantically, trying to face Roscoe.

Roscoe turned slightly and she saw something in his left hand. She heard a pop, then a hiss, and saw a yellow flame come from the brass torch in his right hand. He twisted the knobs on the handle until the yellow disappeared and the flame turned an intense blue. Then he held it to Finn's back and moved it around like he was writing his name.

She saw Finn squirm and then his scream snapped her into action. She spotted a two-foot section of round metal stock lying on the concrete. She grabbed it and ran behind Roscoe, who would not have heard her above Finn's screams and was enjoying himself too much to be distracted.

Emma landed a mighty swing on the boney tip of Roscoe's right shoulder. He yelled and dropped the torch. It clattered to the floor and Roscoe ducked and turned to her, his face contorted in bestial rage. Emma felt her insides go soft. She wound up for another blow, but he was too quick. His backhand across her face sent her body toppling like a tree and she felt the rough floor slide beneath her. The last thing she remembered was the sound of the metal rod bouncing across the concrete.

~

As soon as he heard Roscoe yell and felt the burning pain diminish on his back, Finn knew his chance was now. Someone had come to his rescue. He needed only seconds to free his hands. But he didn't know how long until Roscoe returned with the flame. Finn bent at the waist, reached up and grabbed the steel hook above his feet in both hands. He pulled himself up and over the pulley until he could reach the cable, then pulled hand-over-hand until he was upright, standing on the pulley and out of Roscoe's reach.

Only then did he look down. Emma lay behind him on her back on the concrete. Roscoe stood over her but something made him turn and look up. When he saw Finn out of reach, he clenched his fists and bellowed.

"Think you're a smart, faggot?" Roscoe looked down at Emma. "There's more than one way to catch a monkey."

Finn hurriedly unwound the wire from his ankles. He watched Roscoe drag Emma by one leg to the unlit torch lying on the floor. Panic rose inside him. *He's going to torture her.* Roscoe bent over, picked up the torch in one hand and the igniter in the other. Finn knew he had only seconds until she suffered the scorching flame. He grabbed the control cable and hauled it. A quick glance told him that Roscoe had bent over Emma. Finn held the control box in his hands. He heard the igniter pop and the torch hiss. Emma screamed. He looked again. She was on her back, hands and feet scrambling like a lizard to get away from Roscoe. With his free hand, Roscoe caught and pinned her. *Shit!*

The control cable. The mass of the hook and pulley under his feet would resist him enough to get the distance he needed. He held the control box in both hands, bent his knees, and pushed hard off the pulley, away from Roscoe. Emma screamed. *I'm coming.* Finn arced through the air pulling the cable behind him. It snapped taught with a shoulder wrenching jolt and swung back toward Roscoe. Finn twisted his body to face Roscoe. The flame was almost touching Emma's face.

The cable picked up speed. Finn straightened his legs. Both feet slammed into the back of Roscoe's head. His body sailed over Emma and fell in a crumpled heap on the cement. Finn pulled his knees up to his chest. He swung backwards. The only sounds were the hissing torch and the creaking hoist. He swung forward. Emma was getting to her feet. Another backswing. Emma grabbed the metal bar, stepped quickly to Roscoe and began to bludgeon him in a frenzied fury.

Finn dragged his feet and stopped. He released the cable and ran to Emma. "Hold on."

She swung the bar with vengeance. Her lust for blood might cause her to hit him accidentally.

"Son of a bitch!" she yelled. Roscoe's body bounced with each blow. His head looked like someone had run over a watermelon.

"Emma!"

"Pervert!" she screamed.

Finn timed her movements, stepped in quickly and pinned her arms to her side. "Wait. Let's make sure you're okay."

She didn't take her eyes off Roscoe. "I'm fine. It's this asshole who needs help."

Finn took the metal bar from her hands. "Let's be sure. I'll take you to the hospital."

"No," she finally looked at him. "I don't need a doctor. Take me home."

Finn pointed to the rear door. "We can do that. First, you sit over there. I'll clean this up."

Emma stomped over to the door and dropped to a squat. Her arms clenched across her chest and her lungs filled the quiet shop with the sound of forced breathing. Suddenly, she stood and began pulling at her pee-soaked trousers. "Do you suppose there's a shower somewhere?"

"In the office." Finn pointed to the door with the broken window. "Probably fresh work clothes if you look around."

Finn looked down at Roscoe. It was hard to see any part of his body not covered in blood. Then he moved. One arm slowly disappeared under his body and he began to push himself up from the concrete. Finn was fascinated. How could the man still live with so much damage?

Roscoe rose to his knees and then sat back on his heels. Finn stood behind him. That was far enough. He removed a folding knife from his pocket. The four-inch blade locked open. He stepped beside Roscoe and drove it into the side of his neck. Bright arterial blood squirted from the carotid artery. Roscoe's hands went to his throat and he toppled forward onto his face. This time he lay still.

Finn removed Roscoe's clothes and took everything from the pockets, wallet, iPhone, keys. He found a plastic garbage bag and dumped the clothes into it. The rest he set aside. Then he dragged Roscoe's naked body to the large commercial parts washer and unlatched the door, which opened like a refrigerator, to reveal a round metal turntable at the bottom of a large cabinet lined with high-pressure nozzles. He maneuvered Roscoe's corpse onto the turntable, secured his arms and legs inside, then closed and latched the heavy door.

"What's that going to do?" Emma shouted. She returned from the shower wearing pressed blue coveralls. She had used tin-snips to cut off the legs and now looked like a circus clown in baggy shorts.

"They use this to clean engines and generators and other large pieces of equipment," Finn said while he studied the control panel. "It uses sodium hydroxide. Very corrosive. Think drain cleaner." He made adjustment to the dials on the panel. "I'm setting the temperature and pressure to the max. It will strip the flesh from his bones in no time."

"Then what?"

"We flush Roscoe down the drain."

"Bones too?"

"The alkali weakens them. They crush into powder. When we're finished, you can scatter them in the street if you want."

"Yeah. Let him run into the sewer." Emma sat by the exit door from the annex.

Finn pushed the machine's green start button and the motors, pumps and hoses connected to the cabinet came alive, turning, pulsing, and hissing. He walked slowly to Emma and sat next to her. He put an arm around her shoulders.

"We've got a while before he's cleaned. Then I'll take you home."

Emma leaned her head back on Finn's arm and closed her eyes. "Thank God. What a monster. I had no idea . . ."

He leaned over her and sniffed loudly. "You smell so much better."

"And you look horrible," she said.

Finn guffawed.

"At least I showered."

"Yeah, well. What about Logan?" he whispered. "Won't he come looking?"

"We setup the wire transfer together. He knows the money goes to BrighTel."

Finn sat quietly for several minutes. When he spoke his voice was soft. "I almost got killed."

She tilted her head to hear better.

"He nearly drowned me. He tried to roast me."

She put one hand on his forearm and squeezed gently.

"I would have been killed if you hadn't done whatever you did to distract him," he swallowed.

"He almost roasted me too," she said softly

He looked away. "First man I really wanted to kill."

She moved her head into his line of sight. He could not avoid her eyes or her gentle voice, "I wanted to kill him too. I really did."

Finn was at a loss to explain his elation at having killed Roscoe. He'd refused to kill anyone until now. It had formed a cornerstone of the relationship with Philippe. Yet, a weight had lifted from his shoulders. He'd almost died. Hadn't been 100 percent certain he could defeat Roscoe. Yet here he was. The victor. He felt like he could do anything.

After a while, he turned to Emma, "What now?"

She looked down and studied her hands for a long time. Then, on impulse, she grabbed Finn's left arm and turned it to expose the inside of his wrist. She turned her own left hand, palm up, and held it next to Finn's. They stared wordlessly at the identical tattoos. Finally, she said. "What happened to us, Finn?"

"Things got too intense." He looked out the window. "We talked about it already."

"Yes, but you didn't have to disappear. Not say anything."

"I already told you I couldn't get close."

"You told me your parents died when you were a kid, but I didn't think that meant we could never have a life."

"Guess I never trusted anyone after." He looked at his hands. " My lifestyle didn't help. People coming and going. Every time I liked someone, they'd always disappear." *Or disappoint.*

He felt her hand pull his chin around and she looked into his eyes. "Is it always going to be like that with you?"

Finn looked away from her eyes. "I don't know." He sighed. "Guess I only ever trusted Philippe. But he's gone."

After a short silence, Finn took an iPhone from his trousers and held it out for Emma. "Philippe's. Roscoe had it."

Emma grabbed the phone and her face lit up. "My God, Finn! You have no idea how much this means to me. Thank you." She put the phone in her pocket.

"How did Roscoe get it?"

Her head turned away.

"He must have taken it from Philippe. Said he found him dead." Finn glanced at Emma. She faced away and he saw her dark wet hair. Drops of water landed on his arm when she shook her head.

"Do you suppose Logan sent him there?"

She faced him. "No, Finn. Logan just bought Xanthus, remember? I don't think he had anything to do with Roscoe being in Italy."

He looked deep into her eyes, "What happened to Philippe, Emma?"

She looked away again, slid her hands to her upper arms, and hugged herself. He was surprised by her intense look of regret when she turned to him again. "He was going to leave me. Said I wasn't a suitable wife for the culture where he was going. He was going to take everything."

She killed Philippe. A chilling ache settled in his chest. The power he'd felt just moments ago vanished. His friend was dead. He had protected the killer. *Me. I did it. Imbecile.* The icy pain descended to his abdomen, twisted his intestines. He felt his vitality drain onto the cold concrete.

~

Holliday crushed his last cigarette in the ashtray of the Subaru and wondered what was keeping Roscoe. He'd seen the Corvette parked in front of the annex earlier. It was still here so Roscoe must be inside. The big man had told him to wait in his car. He'd have good news about Xanthus. He'd heard enough bad news from Logan about Xanthus and Roscoe over the last two days. Hopefully, this meeting would signal that Roscoe was sober and back on track. He needed him.

Out of the corner of his eye, Holliday saw the lights go dark inside the annex. Finally. Always cautious, he cracked the driver's door so it wouldn't make any noise if he needed to get out of the car. He was stunned to see Hauken come out of the annex carrying two black garbage bags. Kassar's wife followed him to Roscoe's sports car. She opened the passenger door while Hauken walked to the trunk and stood with his back to Holliday, stowing the bags.

What happened to Roscoe? Holliday pushed open the Subaru's door and stepped silently onto the pavement. His right hand reached into his jacket and withdrew two wooden handles connected by a short length of steel wire. He flew across the road on his toes, half a dozen lightening steps, and was behind Hauken before the man knew he was there.

In one fluid motion, Holliday took a handle in each hand, reached over Hauken's head, pulled the wire taught around his neck, crossed his own hands, and dropped to one knee, pulling Hauken down from behind. Hauken kicked the rear of the car as he fell backward. His hands flew up over his head searching for a hold on his assailant. Holliday kept his other knee in the middle of Hauken's back and rolled him onto his side. There was no way for him to escape. His legs kicked and arms flailed. He tried to turn, but Holliday had him pinned to the ground. He had no concern for the outcome.

He didn't expect to feel someone jump on his back and lock an arm around his own throat. *The wife. Well one thing at a time.* Holliday pulled on the garrote. Once Hauken was unconscious he could deal with Missus Kassar.

"Stop," he heard her say. "Stop it. He didn't kill Younger." Her strangle hold was surprisingly strong and he felt his larynx threatened by her forearm. He began to have his own breathing problems. But he could feel Hauken's strength fade, his struggles growing spasmodic. He would succumb.

"Holliday!" she screamed in his ear. "This is Emma Kassar. Stop it."

Hauken went limp. Holliday needed air. He released the garrote and tried to stand in order to get the woman off his back. As soon as she saw Hauken was free, she let go of Holliday, twisted around him, and dropped beside the unconscious man. She took his head in her hands and looked into his face.

'You better not have killed him," she shouted without looking up.

Holliday stood over the pair while he caught his breath.

"He killed Younger."

Emma looked up. "You idiot! Philippe killed Younger. He told people that Hauken did it so you wouldn't kill him."

Holliday's mouth hung open. "Why would Philippe kill Younger?"

Emma had her hand on Finn's heart. She lowered her face to his nostrils so she could feel his breath on her eyes. After several moments, she looked up at Holliday. "He's breathing." Holliday's expression didn't change. He waited for her to answer his question.

"I don't know why. I just know he did. He sent Finn away so the Chinese wouldn't find him. Since no one knew where he was, he let him take the blame for Younger."

Holliday wasn't sure he believed her. She still held Finn's lifeless face, but looked up at him with pleading eyes.

"Finn was in Malaysia when Younger was killed."

Holliday waived a hand in the air.

"Check his passport."

Holliday confidence waned. He'd held the rage for two years. It wouldn't just vanish. But he could at least move ahead. "Where is Roscoe?"

Emma looked down again at Finn. Holliday watched her set his lifeless head gently on the ground and look back into his eyes.

"He killed my brother, Holliday. He kidnapped me. He beat me. He was going to rape me. I hit him with a metal pipe."

"He is dead then." His face showed no emotion.

She nodded. "I was afraid for my life."

Holliday looked into the distance. So much to give up in one night. But he had no choice. Roscoe had finally gone too far. He gave her a sad smile. "He could be like that." When she said nothing, he furrowed his eyebrows. "This is not what I expected, Missus Kassar. What about Xanthus?"

"It belongs to Logan as of yesterday."

"Well, that is something, at least." He reflected for a moment. "Roscoe went to Italy to talk with Philippe. Unfortunately, your husband was dead when he found him. It made me sad. I liked Philippe. He was good for business."

Finn opened his eyes. Holliday saw his hands move to his throat, feel gingerly around his neck. He coughed then winced from the pain. He sat up and looked at Emma, then at Holliday.

"You must be Holliday." It came out more as a croak. "Heard you were here."

"Yes. For now." He didn't need to say any more to these people. Holliday turned and crossed the street. He got into the green Subaru Forester and drove away thinking about what to do next. *Who can replace Roscoe?* No one came to mind. *Well, at least Xanthus is under my control again. I won't lose my biggest customer. Their secrets will continue to travel in Korea.* Then, he relaxed in the driver's seat and concentrated on finding a convenience store on Third where he could buy cigarettes.

~

The wire had cut Finn's neck and it hurt like hell. The pain in his throat felt more immediate than the scorched skin on his back. He cringed every time he had to swallow. It hurt to speak—if you called a scratchy whisper speaking. The events of the past few hours left him numb. He would have died twice if Emma hadn't saved him. Both times. And he was supposed to be protecting her. Just thinking about it sent a shiver through his body. Yet, she had Philippe killed. He forced himself to concentrate, to ignore anguish as well as the pain in his throat and his back. He leaned forward in the seat and drove the blue Corvette along the divided highway, through the traffic light on Third to Islias Creek Park. He stopped the 'vette next to the concrete dividers that kept errant lovers and drunks away from the water's edge. He shut off the engine and turned to Emma in the passenger seat.

"Do the honors," he whispered.

She got out to the car, retrieved one of the garbage bags from the trunk and came around to the open driver's window. "The whole bag or just the contents?"

"Contents," Finn mouthed.

Emma walked over the rocks to the water's edge, held the black bag upside down, and watched a cold wind carry the powdered remains of Roscoe's skeleton onto the water where it formed a scum on the surface and floated slowly toward the San Francisco Bay.

"Creep," she snorted and shook the bag until it stopped releasing swirls of powder into the wind. Then she returned to the car.

Finn drove them south on Highway 101 to the airport. They wiped down the 'vette. Left it in long-term parking and distributed the remaining garbage bags and contents into various trash containers. They caught the tram to the terminal, boarded BART for the Embarcadero, and collapsed exhausted onto a seat in an empty car. Finn twisted his body to keep his back from touching the upright.

BART stopped at the Embarcadero Station. They exited, took the escalator to the Muni Level, and caught the light rail for Forest Hill station.

They sat together on one seat. Finn left a space between them. There were no other passengers. Finn watched buildings flash by the window. What had he accomplished? Nothing. He could not think of a single thing. Beside him sat the woman who'd killed his only friend. She stared ahead into empty space. Finally, she spoke. "Philippe always told me how beautiful Lebanon was," she straightened in the seat. "I haven't relaxed since he died. Maybe I need a radical change."

"Lebanon?" Finn gave an incredulous laugh then turned his head back to the window. *How will I punish you?*

MONDAY

Dawn brightened the home office in Logan Evan's condo, but he could care less. With growing concern, he studied the computer screen on his desk. He slid his chair closer to the monitor, hoping he might have misread it. Last night's contentment drained rapidly from his mind, replaced by an overwhelming rush of anxiety. He was aware of Myrna behind him, one hand resting on the shoulder of his silk bathrobe.

"What the hell?" Logan cleared his throat. He slid both hands back over his bald head and joined fingers behind his neck. He studied the screen. "Fucking BrighTel! They didn't buy the spectrum?"

"What do you mean?" Myrna's voice had a sharp edge. He felt her hand leave his shoulder.

"Look," he turned to her and pointed back at the monitor. He was incredulous. "They announced the funding. Then they—" He turned to the monitor. "They used it to pay off short-term debt?"

Logan read out loud. "Blah blah blah, now that the firm has fulfilled its obligations to creditors, it intends to restructure operations to focus on satellite television. What the—"

"What's that mean?"

He stared into the screen. "The whole idea was to acquire them before anyone learned they could buy more wireless spectrum. When they own more of the airwaves, which is worth a bundle, their stock shoots through the roof. We sell. We make a fortune."

He turned again to Myrna. The eyes looking back at him were the coldest blue he'd ever seen. He raised his voice. "But those idiots! They pay off their debts, reorganize the business, which is now worth diddle-y-squat. And me—" he paused and calculated his position, "Holy shit!"

"What about Emma?"

"This had nothing to do with her."

"She couldn't have known this would happen?"

"She had nothing to do with BrighTel. Besides, she got her end. "

"Maybe she just wanted to fuck you up."

"Myrna, you're always looking for the worst in people."

"Well, what are you going to do now?"

"We're screwed!"

Myrna stepped away from Logan's chair and he watched her pace around the small office. After a few hesitant steps, her motions seemed to galvanize. She glanced over at him. He saw determination. She grabbed her handbag and jacket from a nearby chair and headed for the front door.

"Myrna, wait."

She didn't turn her head, but he heard the ice in her voice. "Goodbye Logan." He watched her yank open the door. She came face to face with a man in a dark suit, his hand poised to knock. A second man, identically dressed, stood behind him. The three of them froze in surprise. Myrna recovered first.

"And fuck you too," she said. "Whoever you are." She straightened her back and sauntered around them down the hallway. Logan sat speechless in his chair. The two men looked at each other and shrugged. The lead man turned to the open door and addressed him. "Logan Evans?"

Logan nodded.

"May we come in?"

Logan nodded again, mindless. The two men entered the condo and closed the door. *What the hell?* Logan asked himself. *My life has turned to shit and . . . Who are these guys?* He watched the first man remove a folded paper from the inside breast pocket of his suit. With his other hand he pulled a wallet from his trousers and flipped it open. Logan saw the ID and gold badge.

"I'm agent Bonaventure. This is agent Ruppert of the Bureau of Industry and Security." Ruppert stepped forward and held out his credentials for Logan to see.

Logan stood up, examined their IDs. "What's this about? And what's the Bureau of Industry and Security?"

"We're part of the Department of Commerce." Ruppert said.

"We understand you're a partner in Xanthus Investments," Bonaventure said.

"I'm the owner." Logan said without pride.

"We have the owner as one Philippe Kassar." Bonaventure exchanged an uncertain glance with Ruppert.

"Kassar died last week. I'm now the sole owner."

Bonaventure nodded to Ruppert. "No wonder he didn't respond." He looked back at Logan. "Xanthus is in violation of the Arms Export Control Act. This is a cease and desist order." He flipped open the folded paper and held it out. "It means the company cannot do business as of this moment."

Logan grabbed the paper and read. "Xanthus doesn't do arms shipments," he said without looking up.

"Apparently it does," Ruppert countered. "Xanthus shipped integrated circuits made by a smartphone manufacturer in California to a competitor in South Korea."

"What, Apple? Samsung?" Logan squinted at the agent.

Bonaventure gave him a condescending smile. "Just know that transfer of the technology is restricted."

Logan's jaw fell open. "You're talking about stuff that will be in the hands of the general public in a few months."

Ruppert took over. "The circuits in question were prototypes. They operate at clock frequencies that exceed the limits specified in the The Commerce Control List. They were never intended to leave the company. Someone acquired them illegally and Xanthus shipped them to Korea without obtaining the required licensees."

"It's dual-use technology," Bonaventure added. "Military and civilian applications."

"That's ridiculous," Logan's face reddened. "We just lost millions on a telecom deal and you want me to worry about an export license?" His day was getting worse. *If that was possible.*

"Would you mind getting dressed?" Bonaventure said. "We'd like you to come with us."

Logan's feet wouldn't move. He stood by his desk. His face was ashen. Images of prison bars, striped pajamas, and big men with homemade knives shot through his mind. He gaped at the agent and with one hand he pointed to the monitor behind him. His hand trembled. He stammered, "But . . . but, it's not even worth anything."

~

Hedges picked up Allegra from her hotel. He had a mocha waiting for her in the car.

"Sorry we did not find Mister Pender or Mister Hauken last night," she said when she got in.

"Never mind," he said. "Xanthus is holding a press conference this morning. We'll look for them there."

Hedges drove to 101 California and was pleasantly surprised to find parking in front of the Davis Street entrance near the corner of Pine Street. Allegra had been talking on her mobile in Italian for most of the drive. While she continued, he studied the crowd of pedestrians entering the building. After several minutes, Allegra closed her phone and looked at Hedges with an expression of triumph.

"Romero find man who fix murder of Mister Kassar." Her eyes shone.

"Good news," Hedges said.

"Romero also say this man tell him *teppisti* who kill Mister Kassar leave Italy."

"That's no good."

"*Si*. Is no good. You think they come to America?"

Before he could answer, Hedges spotted Hauken and Emma approaching along Market Street from his left. "Look." He pointed. "Let's catch some killers of our own." They both opened their doors and stood by the car.

~

Finn stepped into the crosswalk on Davis Street and came to a sudden standstill when he spotted the detective and the blond woman waiting by a cruiser on the far side of the street. Emma looked at him to see why he'd stopped. By the time she'd followed his glance, Hedges had jogged over and grabbed Finn's right arm.

"Let's have a word, hot shot," he said and escorted Finn back across the street onto a patio outside the lobby of 101 California.

"Detective," Emma, hurrying on Finn's left, had to lean in front of him to address Hedges. "What are you doing?'

"It's okay," Finn told her.

"We need to talk," Hedges said, stopping between a pair of large concrete tubs filled with drooping ferns, but keeping a steady grip on Finn's elbow. Hedges' back was to the street. Allegra followed them onto the patio and stood between Finn and Emma, facing Hedges on the opposite side of the tight circle.

Allegra looked at Emma on her left. "Roscoe go into room where Philippe die. Our laboratory match his DNA to—" she glanced at Hedges for help, "*Vomito?*"

"Barf," he said.

"Barf, *si. Pasta con tartufo.* How you say, truffle."

"Saw Philippe dead and barfed?" Finn guffawed.

"Not a heavyweight," Hedges said.

Finn smiled at Hedges. "There you go. Case closed."

"Not so fast," Hedges said.

Allegra stared at Emma. "No. Three people go into room. Two before Roscoe. Footprints tell us story."

"Finn's not a suspect," Emma directed a confidant gaze toward Finn.

Hedges turned to Emma on his right. "Let's just say he's a person of interest."

"But you have warrant for murder of Younger Park," Allegra looked curiously at Hedges.

Now, Emma looked at Hedges. "That's ridiculous. He wasn't even in the country when Younger died. Check his passport."

"What she is saying?" Allegra asked.

Hedges saw it would get complicated. He used his calming baritone. "You know what? This is not the place. Let's all go downtown where we can sort this out."

"But he didn't kill anyone," Emma objected.

"Signora Kassar, you will come with us also." Allegra held her hand out to Emma.

"What? Me?" Emma took a step backward. "No."

"Perhaps you say why someone make assault on your husband," Allegra's tone was firm.

"I don't know anything about that," Emma's expression grew cold.

It was Hedges turn to regard Allegra with a puzzlement. "What are you talking about?"

"I just was going to tell you," Allegra said. "The man Romero caught tell him woman hire him to kill her husband."

Finn turned to Emma, saw her expression tighten. She stared hard at Allegra for several seconds. Then gave her a nervous smile, turned, and marched up Davis Street.

Hedges guffawed and called after her, "Missus Kassar."

Emma didn't break stride. Finn saw Hedges signal for Allegra to stay beside him and heard Emma's steps grow more determined.

"Come back, Missus Kassar." Hedges moved quickly, an enormous gait for a stout man, and caught her arm. "Not so fast. Running makes you look awfully guilty."

Emma faced Hedges with fire in her eyes. "I don't know what you're talking about."

In the periphery of his vision, Finn saw a short dark man dash from behind one of the building support columns by the lobby door and race toward Emma. At the same time, he heard purposeful footsteps behind him. He turned his head left and saw a fat man marching toward Allegra with his right arm extended before him, the hand pointing a semiautomatic pistol at her head.

Finn dove to his left at the fat man. Concern for Emma flashed in his mind and then vanished. His right hand hit the fat man's gun arm from below and knocked it skyward. The weapon flew in the air. He fell into the assailant and they landed on the pavement, Finn on top, face down. He heard a clatter when the automatic hit the concrete and then a shot. He felt a rush of panic.

Finn rolled over quickly, expecting the worst. Allegra stood unharmed a few feet away and to his left. Directly in front of him, Hedges fell to his side on the pavement. The dark man held Emma like a shield before him, one arm around her waist, the other pointing a smoking pistol at Hedges.

The dark assailant moved his gun to Emma's temple. The fat man's gun lay on the concrete by Allegra. Finn rolled toward it and knew the motion would attract the dark man's attention. He snatched the automatic off the pavement and brought it up just as the dark man fired in his direction. Sharp stings bit into his face, arms, and chest. The bullet had struck the pavement. He fired without thought.

A smudge appeared on the dark man's forehead and he collapsed like a broken marionette. Emma stood stiff, frozen in shock. Finn rolled to his stomach, looking for the fat man. He lay where he had fallen. Finn stood and walked to the fat man, pulled him up by the front of his jacket, and stuck the automatic under his nose.

"Who the fuck are you?" Finn's eyes glowed with rage.

"*Non capito.*" The man's expression was defiant. Finn jerked him by the collar, drug him to a spot beside Hedges, who now lay on his back. Allegra bent over the detective and opened his suit coat. Blood oozed from the left side of his shirt. Allegra removed her scarf and pressed it firmly on the wound.

Finn pushed the fat man into a sitting position. He took the cuffs from Hedges' belt and shackled the man's feet together. Then he turned to the detective.

"Didn't they teach you to get out of the way?"

Hedges had been studying the prone corpse. Now he turned and gave him a frown. "Where'd you learn to shoot like that?"

"My ill spent youth." Hedges looked confused. "Small circus. Did everything. Tumbling. Clowning. High wire. Houdini stuff. And my favorite: shooting cigarettes from the lips of beautiful women."

Hedges tried to sit. Finn watched him grimace and fall back to the pavement. He took a deep breath. "I'm okay. Meat wagon's on its way."

"You want me to stick around? Hold your hand?"

"Yeah, wise ass." Hedges eyes searched for Emma. "Both of you. We'll sort it out downtown."

"You won't be doing much sorting for a while."

"Then my associate. I believe you'd prefer to sort with her anyway."

Finn smiled and stood up. He walked over to Emma, still dazed from the shock of seeing Finn shoot a gun at her head.

"You almost shot me." Her outrage was palpable.

"No, I didn't."

"He was inches away, Finn!"

"You're still alive." His voice was calm. "And no one's holding a gun to your head."

"Oh, right," she nodded toward Hedges lying on the pavement. "Big Dick there wants to lock me away."

The sound of sirens grew louder. The paramedics came and loaded Hedges onto a gurney and wheeled him to an ambulance.

Allegra walked up and addressed him. "You are good man, signore Hauken. You save my life. Thank you. Now we must go to station." She gestured for Emma to go first, "Missus Kassar." She escorted them to a squad car. After they were seated in the back, Finn turned to Emma. "You had my friend, your husband, killed. Then used me to help you get away with it."

He was stunned to see a smirk on her face. "Everyone uses you, Finn. You're afraid of people. They see it. Even Philippe used you. You were his boy from day one. Did everything he asked. And how did he repay you? He killed Younger Park and told Holliday you killed him to save his own ass. Your friend? Hah!"

Finn's cheeks burned. He didn't look at Emma. *Philippe killed Younger? And he blamed me?* Finn's vision blurred. He lost his bearings. To steady himself, he concentrated on watching the uniformed policeman and paramedics flooding into the plaza.

He was startled to feel Emma reach into his pants pocket. "Keep this," she whispered. Her hand withdrew and a flat object pressed against his thigh.

She raised her eyebrows and gave him an intense, purposeful stare.

"There's a file called, *Biblos*. It's in French, but you'll figure it out. Follow the directions, then come get me out of jail, if I'm still there, otherwise at home.

"Biblos?"

"Ancient Phoenician port. About an hour north of Beirut. Philippe's family home. It's all in the file. Contacts. Account numbers. Take what you need. I know you'll do the right thing."

He let his hand drop to his side and felt the iPhone in the pocket of his trousers. The cold ache he'd felt earlier settled again in his chest. *She's buying me off.*

To his right, he saw Allegra standing by the open door, regarding him. "In America, you have many good lawyer. I think you do not go to jail."

Finn stared into her eyes, into the space beyond and thought of how wrong he'd been about Emma, about Philippe. They'd run his life. Them and others. What had he gained? Where was he now? Sitting in the back of a squad car. Suddenly his focus returned to the plane of Allegra's face. He saw compassion and affection in her twinkling eyes. A balm to his soul.

Finn reached into his pocket. He turned the iPhone over in his hand. Philippe grinned at him from the screen saver. *Traitor.* He held the phone out for Allegra to take.

"Finn!" Emma shouted and reached for the phone. He moved it out of her reach.

"Finn, don't." He ignored her.

"What is this?" Allegra took the phone. Her eyes widened in surprise or suspicion, Finn couldn't tell.

"Everything you need to wrap up your investigation."

Allegra stared down at the phone for a moment. Recognition crossed her face. She nodded, then she stepped back and closed the car door. She reached out and touched the glass, called to him, "No escape this time."

Finn looked at her and winked. Her face lit up. He sat back in the seat. She wasn't going anywhere

ANOTHER DAY

Finn lounged on the deck outside the twenty-eight-foot Airstream, enjoying the warmth of the late afternoon sun. He lay in the recliner with his eyes closed. The smell of oak and manzanita was comforting, the tamari almonds were crunchy, the white wine, cool to his pallet. Only the niggling feeling of someone watching made his eyes open. He turned his head to the left.

"Hauken, you killed my business." He looked into the expressionless face of Holliday Park. *How had he walked to the deck and taken a seat without me or Mattie hearing?* He chose to remain still.

"Only thing I killed was Roscoe and he got what he deserved. How's that killing your business?"

"He was going to run Xanthus. You killed him. An inconvenience, but not insurmountable. However, Logan's now in jail. Xanthus is finished. I lost my best customers."

"Not all together my fault."

"I can get them back. I just need to start up again."

"So start. What's keeping you?" Finn lifted his head to look Holliday in the eye.

"This business needs to be owned by a US citizen."

Finn sensed where this was going. He waited.

"You did a good job for Philippe. He liked you. I believe I could trust you to do an even bigger job for me."

"You tried to kill me. Twice."

"Yes. Because I thought you killed Younger. Now, I know better. Apologies. I hope you can overlook the error."

Finn saw a frank sincerity in Park's eyes. He thought about the offer. "I don't know anything about the business. Just what Philippe told me."

"I'm sure you could do it, Finn Hauken. And it will make you wealthy."

Finn let his head fall back to the recliner and closed his eyes. He took a deep breath. Let the woody smell of oak and manzanita fill his lungs. *User.* Popped into his head. *Traitor.* He opened his eyes and looked at Holliday.

"I respectfully decline."

Finn was surprised. Holliday's expression remained unchanged. He simply nodded and stood up. He dropped a business card on the low table beside Finn. "You would do very well in this business and you would make a lot of money, Finn Hauken. Call me by the end of the week if you change your mind."

Holliday disappeared from Finn's sight without a sound. Behind him, he heard the screen door open.

"Who is guest?" Allegra's voice hung in the summer heat.

Finn turned, saw her warmhearted interest. He smiled and held out his hands. "A guy from the circus. I told him, no more tightropes."

ACKNOWLEDGEMENTS

Hanna K. Jones improved this story's focus and continuity with talented editing. I am grateful for her caring and insightful criticism. Any mistakes or inaccuracies in the text are mine alone.

www.ingramcontent.com/pod-product-compliance
Lightning Source LLC
Chambersburg PA
CBHW030640130626
46552CB00002B/940